PRAISE FOR KAT SIMONS' TIGER SHIFTERS

Once Upon a Tiger

"This is a novel of passion long denied. That banked passion is a flickering flame about to become a raging forest fire. You will be panting yourself before the book ends. [...] Readers will enjoy reading this page turner."

—*Night Owl Reviews*

"I really enjoyed this riveting introduction to a new world of tiger shifters with its interesting concepts and bewitching characters. I just with it had been a little longer because it ended way too fast."

—*The Romance Reviews*

"This is the first book in the...series, and I enjoyed it immensely. [...] I really want to read the next book of this series to see how Ms. Simons grows this universe."

—*The Romance Studio*

"Victor's backstory broke my heart. What an amazing guy! No wonder Alexis was mad for him [...] I was surprised at how much story Ms. Simons was able to fit into so few pages, and I'm hoping this is the start of something bigger. I'd sure like to see more of this crew. Well done!"

—*Long and Short Reviews*

Along Came a Tiger

"…a story with memorable characters and a storyline that keeps you glued to your seat from the beginning to end. […] If you like paranormal romances dealing with shifters then you are going to love Kat [Simons'] Along Came a Tiger."

—*Night Owl Reviews*, TOP PICK

Here There Be Tigers

"The whole book was spellbinding and I was absorbed in the story."

—*Night Owl Reviews*, TOP PICK

Her Tiger to Take

"This is a great read for those like me who want strong characters who feel real and are written in a way that you feel an emotional connection and empathy with as they work to be together."

—*The Romance Reviews*, TOP PICK

To Tempt a Tiger

"I definitely want to stay involved in this world and visit more of the couples and their friends and family."

—*The Romance Reviews*, TOP PICK

"The chemistry is a smoldering inferno of heat but this relationship is slow burning because of personal demons and emotional distress and these strong, compelling characters draw readers in and capture their hearts…The well written scenes and details capture the imagination and bring the story to life while the intriguing events keep readers glued to the pages."

—*Night Owl Reviews*

"These are the types of characters you don't see often and they are anything but predictable….Together, they work to get the justice they have sought for so long and find a love they never expected. It is a story of loss and pain but also hope and second chances. The characters are complex and intriguing and will stay with you long after you finish the story."

—*The Romance Reviews*

Titles by Kat Simons

Tiger Shifters

ONCE UPON A TIGER
ALONG CAME A TIGER
HERE THERE BE TIGERS
HER TIGER TO TAKE
TO TEMPT A TIGER
DOWN WILL COME TIGER

ALONG CAME A TIGER

Tiger Shifter

KAT SIMONS

ALONG CAME A TIGER

Published 2014 by T&D Publishing

Interior book design © 2016 T&D Publishing

ISBN-13: 978-1-944600-01-3

First printing: June 2016

For information, contact T&D Publishing www.TandDPublishing.com

To all my boys.

Acknowledgements

As always, I'd like to thank my husband and my boys for giving me time to write and for giving me an excuse to stop writing so I can play. To those who've supported and helped with my writing career, I can't thank you enough. But I'll try. Thank you: Kemberlee Shortland, Stacey Agdern, Leanna Renee Hieber, Mala Bhattacharjee, Hope Tarr, Elizabeth K. Mahone, Lise Horton, Stacey Klemstein, Linnea Sinclair, and Louise Fury. Many more people have helped me in my publishing journey, to those I didn't name directly, know I appreciate everything you do for me and I thank you from the bottom of my heart. I'd like to thank my parents and sister for everything from babysitting to buying my books. You guys are truly the best. Last, but by no means least, I'd like to thank the readers who have embraced the Tiger Shifters. Thank you all so much! I hope you'll continue to enjoy their stories.

ALONG CAME A TIGER

Tiger Shifters

KAT SIMONS

Chapter One

Ridley Creek State Park outside Philadelphia

Daniel Borowski stared through the darkness at the sleek black Jaguar parked in front of an isolated home at the edge of the park. The bastard with Sarah sat sideways, his profile visible through the back window. Daniel had no trouble discerning Bradley Williams' dark blond hair and blue eyes, even in the dark. Tiger-shifter eyesight was handy that way. He only saw the back of Sarah Chu's head, but he knew it was her.

He'd know Sarah anywhere.

His lip curled as he watched the two. Bradley was the kind of slick, rich asshole who always set Daniel's teeth on edge, but this man's pretty boy exterior hid a murdering evil that sent Daniel's instincts into overdrive. Especially when the bastard was sitting next to Sarah.

Daniel dug his fingers into the bark of a fallen tree in front of him, trying to rein in his anger.

"You're sure you don't need help?" Alexis Tarasova asked from beside him.

He kept his gaze on the car, swallowing a growl as Bradley touched Sarah's cheek.

"I'll be fine," he answered in a tight murmur, hoping his mentor wouldn't pick up on the rage he heard in his own voice. Alexis might have been retired for ten years, but she was still one of the best Trackers he'd ever known. He was a better Tracker for her training. Sometimes, though, her perception was inconvenient. Right now, he needed her to concentrate on her part of this situation, not his straining control. "It'll take both of you to keep Joseph away."

He glanced at her, taking in her focused stare. Beside her, her husband Victor Romanov waited so silently Daniel might have forgotten he was there, if he couldn't sense him.

To the west, not far from their position in the trees surrounding the front of the house, Daniel also sensed Joseph Bennett in his tiger form, waiting for his chance at revenge against the man who'd killed his sister. Joseph was so full of rage he wasn't thinking straight.

Neither was Sarah.

Daniel looked back to the car in time to see the bastard lean toward Sarah and say something close to her ear. Daniel snarled.

Alexis nudged his arm. "Victor can handle Joseph if you need me. The point is *not* to kill the human."

"I haven't forgotten why we're here."

"You sure? Because you're stripping bark off that log."

Daniel scowled down at his hand. His fingers were buried in the thick bark. Fuck. If he couldn't calm his temper, he would ruin everything. He was a Tracker. He should be able to control himself.

For Sarah's sake, he *had* to control himself.

"I'll be fine. Just make sure Joseph doesn't get anywhere near that man. You have a place to…hold him until he's thinking straight again?"

Alexis signed something to her husband, who signed back. Daniel didn't understand sign language so he waited for Alexis to finish.

"We'll take him to Victor's retreat near the Canadian border. That should be far enough from Philly to keep him out of trouble."

Alexis narrowed her eyes and her mouth tightened. The reaction was telling.

"You don't think he'll calm down, do you?" Daniel asked, facing the car again.

"Would you if Williams had murdered your sister?"

"No." He'd want to rip out the man's throat and drink his blood. He was already itching to tear him to pieces, and that was just for *touching* Sarah. He could only imagine what Joseph felt.

Or Sarah for that matter. Su-jin had been her best friend. Sarah's rage and need for revenge no doubt matched Joseph's— strong enough for her to risk her own life.

Among their people, killing a human being, especially in tiger form, was an automatic death sentence. There had been a few exceptions over the years, but that was before forensic science had improved so significantly.

There would be no leniency for Joseph, even given the circumstances. Killing a human risked exposing them all to the human world. Their people were already on the brink of extinction and desperately struggling to survive. They couldn't afford for the general human population to learn that tiger shapeshifters existed.

Sarah might not be put to death because she was a rare female tiger, but she would be caged for life if she went through with this. Daniel couldn't allow that. He loved her too much to let her to throw her life away.

"He's getting closer," Daniel said, jerking his head in the direction of Joseph's approach.

A soft growl carried through the dense woods, quiet enough only the tigers would be able to hear it. The enraged tiger knew they were there to stop him and he was warning them off.

Alexis glanced at Victor, then back at Daniel. "Good luck. Keep her safe."

Daniel nodded and watched as she and Victor slipped into the darkness under the trees. As they disappeared, he glimpsed Victor begin to disrobe. He would shift into his tiger shape while Alexis stayed in human form. Between them, they'd be able to handle Joseph, no matter how angry the man was. At least Daniel hoped so. As a former Tracker, Alexis had handled worse. But Joseph was Victor's best friend. They'd try not to hurt him.

Daniel focused on the car again. Joseph was their responsibility. He had to trust Alexis and Victor to do their part. His job right now was to get Sarah out of this, unharmed. And to avoid killing the bastard with her.

He pulled in a deep breath, letting the warm, humid summer air clear his head. The scent of beech, oak, fresh cut grass, and soil settled him. He waited and listened to the others as they closed with Joseph. Then he rose from his hiding spot beside the drive and approached the car on Sarah's side. The gravel covered driveway barely crunched under his light footsteps.

He snatched open Sarah's door before Williams realized Daniel was there. Sarah, on the other hand, glared up at him. He knew she'd felt him approach. Hell, she'd known he was in the trees.

For a split second, the dark power of her gaze stilled him. Even angry, she was the most beautiful woman he'd ever known. Black straight hair hung over her shoulders. The car's interior light threw shadows across her sharp features, highlighting high cheekbones and the beautiful tilt of her dark brown eyes. Without thought, his gaze dropped to her mouth— those full lips had always captivated him. Right now, they were pressed tight together, and her jaw was clenched.

He blinked and forced himself to remember why he was here.

"Out," he ordered. "Now. We're leaving."

"Who the hell are you?" Williams demanded.

"Her fiancé," Daniel easily lied. As far as he was concerned, it was only a partial lie anyway.

"You shouldn't be here," Sarah hissed.

This close, the smell of Bradley Williams' lust and strangeness punched at Daniel. Though it was a subtle texture, impossible for Daniel to describe in human words, he could tell from Williams' scent the man wasn't sane, and his lust wasn't for sex.

Despite Daniel's best effort to control his temper, he snarled, a low animal sound rising in his throat. He swallowed down the instinctive challenge and reached a hand out to Sarah.

She ignored it. "It's none of your business what I do," she said.

"This *is* my business."

"You heard the lady," Williams said. "She wants to be here. Looks like your engagement is off. Beat it."

Daniel kept his gaze on Sarah so his tiger didn't get the best of him. He quickly unfastened her seatbelt and pulled her from the car. "I understand why," he whispered into her ear. "Believe me. I understand, but it will only hurt you. I will not allow that."

She jerked free of his hold as soon as her feet were under her. "What I do is not up to you, Daniel."

Williams jumped from the car, slamming his door shut behind him. "What the hell do you think you're doing? Do you have any idea who I am? I will have you thrown in jail for this."

The irony of that comment almost made Daniel laugh. He finally looked the other man in the face, letting him see his anger, and his animal.

Williams stopped short. Some small part of him was sane enough to recognize death when he faced it. Unfortunately, he wasn't sane enough or afraid enough to let that knowledge stop him for long.

"The lady wants to be with me," Williams said with a smirk. "If you don't get the fuck out of here, I'll make sure you're ruined."

"I'll leave right now. With Sarah." He looked down at her. She was a foot shorter than his 6'3", but her stature belied her stubborn will. He scented her anger, a complex acrid punch overlaying her natural scent, and he knew she'd fight him. He couldn't blame her wanting to kill Williams, but throwing away her life for revenge wasn't an option.

"Daniel…" she warned, the quiet edge of tiger in her voice.

He put his face close to hers, their noses almost touching. "I'm not leaving without you."

When she didn't respond, he gripped her arm and started toward the trees, and the path that would take them off Williams' property back to the side road where Daniel had parked his truck. She jerked her arm, trying to pull free, but he refused to let go.

Suddenly, Williams was in front of them, grabbing Daniel's arm in a solid, strong grip and stopping him and Sarah in their tracks. The man's strength and quickness were impressive for a human. Surprisingly so.

Despite Williams' best efforts, though, Daniel refused to drop his hold on Sarah. Whatever strength the man's psychosis gave him, he wasn't strong enough to beat an angry male tiger in a contest of wills.

"Let her go, asshole. Or I swear…"

"What?" Daniel asked, his voice low.

"You won't want to live when I get done with you."

Daniel stared into Williams' eyes and saw just how crazy he was. A deep, dark insanity robbed him of any humane qualities. If Daniel had been a human man, maybe even a less well-trained tiger, he might have been scared. After all, this man had succeeded in capturing, torturing, and killing one of their people—no mere human woman, but a tiger with speed, strength, and rapid healing far outstripping any human.

Granted, Su-jin wasn't as strong as most tigers, but even the weakest of their people could overpower a single human. Most of the time. That this man had held her against her will meant he wasn't to be taken lightly.

A growl lodged in Daniel's throat. He forced down the need to meet Williams' challenge, though every instinct screamed at him to attack and kill the human. Especially because Williams was a threat to Sarah. Daniel couldn't afford to answer the threat. The point of being here was to get Sarah away without either of them killing the human.

He held the man's stare without responding and waited for him to let go.

In the distance, Daniel heard the sounds of a tiger fight—at least one side of it. Victor was mute in both human and tiger form, so there was only the sound of Joseph's chuffs and growls.

Williams' eyes narrowed, as if he detected the noise coming from the woods, too, and Daniel, once again, had to re-evaluate the man still holding his arm. Those sounds should have been too quiet for a human to hear. There was more to Bradley Williams than was apparent, even to acute tiger senses.

"We're leaving now," Daniel said. "It would be best if you backed off."

Williams finally let go with a snarl. "You're a dead man. You messed with the wrong guy." He looked around Daniel and smiled at Sarah. "I'll call you, baby."

Daniel hoped the look he gave William told him if he went anywhere near Sarah again, he'd regret it.

Williams met his look without flinching. "You and I will be seeing each other soon."

Daniel bit his tongue. Every instinct, every fiber of his being, wanted to rip this man apart, to tear through flesh and bone until there was nothing left but bloody pieces. Only the feel of Sarah's warm skin in his hand kept him from acting— remembering he was here to save her from doing something rash.

"Don't call her again," he said through clenched teeth. Then he jerked Sarah into motion and stalked into the trees.

Chapter Two

Over the faint sounds of their passage through the sparse undergrowth, Daniel listened carefully for the human they'd left behind. The hairs on his neck rose as he anticipated an attack, but none came.

Despite her earlier protests, Sarah stopped resisting his hold, allowing him to guide her through the trees. Her cooperation put him on alert. She wouldn't give in this easily. Like Victor and Alexis would have to do with Joseph, Daniel would have to keep her somewhere safe until he could talk sense into her.

Unfortunately, while the others could stay at Victor's retreat for as long as it took, Daniel didn't have that luxury with Sarah. She was less than four days away from her estrous. He couldn't keep her from the Mate Run without raising questions. Questions he wasn't prepared to answer because they could get both Sarah and Joseph locked away for years "for their own good".

He had to convince her to give up her need for revenge, or at least find another way to get it, because killing Williams was not an option.

As they approached Daniel's truck, he listened for traffic on the side road. Only the faint whoosh of cars on the distant highway reached him. One less thing to worry about. They reached the truck without Williams following, and Daniel allowed himself a moment to relax his guard.

Then anger and fear for what could have happened reared. He spun Sarah to face him and took her face between his palms. "I don't want you anywhere near that psycho again. Do you understand me? If he was able to kill Su-jin, he could kill you."

Daniel's heartbeat hammered. Sarah had been alone with that man. What if Daniel hadn't reached her in time? What if he hadn't learned of her and Joseph's plan? What if Williams had done to Sarah what he'd done to Su-jin?

The thought shot a bolt of terror through Daniel so strong he could barely breathe.

"He deserves to die for what he did," Sarah said, her eyes narrowed to slits, her voice rough with emotion.

She trembled with rage. He couldn't blame her for that, but knowing the danger she'd been in swamped him, overwhelming every other sensation, even his own anger.

"Yes, he does," he murmured. "But we have to let the humans take care of him. Do you understand?"

"No! No, I don't. He killed one of *our* people and we let it go? We let him get away with it? Do you know what he did to her, Daniel?"

"Yes, damn it, yes. I know exactly what he did to her."

Rage and fear made his own voice tight. He'd been charged with recovering Su-jin's body from the morgue before the humans could do their autopsy. He knew first hand exactly how much Bradley had tortured her. And in that moment, all he could think about was that very thing happening to Sarah. His chest tightened along with his hands on her face. He had to work to relax his muscles.

Sarah was alive and safe now. He rubbed his thumbs gently along her cheekbones, affirming her skin was warm and she was okay.

Tears filled her eyes. "How can you let him go?"

Her tears tore at Daniel and churned his emotions into a completely different kind of pain. "Oh, love." He pulled her against him, wrapping his arms around her. "I would like nothing more than to break him into little pieces. If he were a tiger, he'd already be dead."

For just an instant, she let him comfort her. For just a breath, she softened in his arms. He closed his eyes and absorbed the sense of rightness he always felt with her.

Then she jerked away, forcing him to drop his hold.

She swiped at the tears leaking across her cheeks. "I want him *dead*."

"I know." And he did. More than she would ever understand. "But I want *you* alive."

Before she could do anything rash, like bolt back toward Willams' house, Daniel lifted her into his arms.

She grunted and smacked him on the shoulder. "What the hell are you doing? Put me down."

Instead, he adjusted his hold on her so he could open the truck door, then he set her inside, fastening the seatbelt around her while she continued glowering at him.

"I'm not a fucking child."

"Believe me; I'm very well aware of that." Though he'd made the effort to keep his attention on the situation, he allowed himself to finally look her over.

She wore a tight dark-colored tank top that revealed the soft swell of her breasts, the curve of her waist, and tight blue jeans that accented the sexy but slight flare of her hips. She was a small, slim woman, almost delicate looking. But he knew for a fact the strength and passion beneath her seeming delicacy. She might appear easily breakable, but for the last seven Runs, she'd taken everything he'd had to give and returned it. With Sarah, looks were deceiving.

His gaze lingered on her lips as memories of their last Run danced through his mind. Sarah naked and laughing as she ducked behind a tree, teasing him, letting him get just close enough to almost grab her before spinning away and racing through the forest. The satisfaction he felt when he out maneuvered her. Her squeal of pretend shock when he caught her. The way she melted against him, hot and eager, as he lifted her off her feet and kissed her. Her smile against his mouth. The spicy flavor of her tongue tangling with his.

She licked her lips, and Daniel almost groaned aloud. He dragged his gaze from her mouth to look her in the eyes. She blinked, the tears no longer falling, something besides sadness and anger in her expression. Her scent curled up around him, floral and spice, with an extra sweet tang of desire.

Without meaning to, he leaned closer, the need to kiss her, to assure himself she was safe and alive was so strong he couldn't resist. He felt the brush of her hot breath on his mouth before he realized what he was doing. Still, he didn't back off immediately because he couldn't make himself give up her nearness, her heat.

He settled his hands on the doorframe with some half-formed intention of pushing back. Instead, the leverage gave him room to move closer, to let his lips just touch hers. So soft…

In the distance, the sound of a passing car broke through his haze and reality punched him back to the moment. What the fuck was he doing? They were still too close to Williams' house for this. Besides, he wasn't even supposed to be with her outside the Run. Kissing her would be a dangerous mistake. Because if he started anything now, he wasn't sure he'd be able to stop at just a kiss.

With a grunt, he pushed away and closed her door very gently, his control stretched to its breaking point. Then he walked around the truck, clenching and unclenching his fists in an attempt to calm his emotions. He slid in behind the wheel and took a few deep breaths.

A mistake. Inside the closed confines of the cabin, her scent wrapped around him with a tighter hold, and the smell of her desire mingling with his almost destroyed him. He closed his eyes, but it was useless. He couldn't resist the temptation to face her.

His gaze lowered to her breasts again, remembering the feel of them against his palms, the taste of them in his mouth. His palms warmed with the phantom feel of her, and it took every ounce of his willpower not to reach out and touch her. When he looked up, her lips were damp and slightly parted, her breathing heavy and deep. His groan slipped out and his hands clenched so tight his fingernails dug into his palms.

Dangerous. Being with her, alone, now…so very, very dangerous.

They needed to get on the road, to get away from this place. He desperately needed the distraction of driving. But he didn't start the car for another long, tense moment as he held her gaze and let her scent wash through him.

Finally, he faced the road, blinking away the haze of lust. Damn his lack of control. This wasn't the time or place. She was angry and hurting. He was here to keep her from destroying her life by taking revenge—or worse, getting herself killed by a crazy man. And they were outside the Run. He risked any hope of a future with her if he gave in to his desires now.

If they still had any hope of a future after tonight.

She might hate him for preventing her from taking revenge. Something he would have to deal with. Right now, his priority was protecting her—from herself, from that psycho Williams, even from Daniel's own needs. Her safety, her life was the important thing now.

He strapped himself in, cranked over the motor, threw the truck into gear, and drove toward the highway. She was going to be even more pissed when she discovered he had no intention of taking her home to her Philadelphia apartment.

The next few days weren't going to be easy. Talking her out of trying to kill Williams was always going to be difficult, but the job was made worse by the fact that Daniel understood her need for revenge. On a visceral level, he actually agreed with her. Williams deserved to die, and they should be the ones to kill him.

When Daniel had broken into the morgue to recover Su-jin Lee-Bennett's body, the sight of her, the damage done to her poor body…he had never felt rage like that before. The only thing that could have made it worse was if it had been Sarah on the slab.

Even the idea of that made his throat close and his blood pressure rise. If that man had killed Sarah, had tortured her in the same way he had Su-jin, Daniel *knew* he wouldn't stop until he'd ripped out Williams' throat—Daniel's job as an enforcer of tiger law be damned. The last eight years of upholding his people's rules, all the good he'd done as a Tracker, would mean nothing to him if Sarah were murdered.

So, how could he ask her, sincerely, to let go of her own anger and give up on killing the man? How could they expect Joseph to forget about revenge when it was *his* only sister who had been murdered?

Daniel didn't have an easy answer to those questions. He only knew he loved Sarah—even if he hadn't admitted it to her—and he did not want her locked away for life. He would do anything to keep her safe. Anything.

He risked a glance at her. She stared out the side window, silent and distant. The thought of losing her punched him in the chest. But he couldn't let that fear stand in his way. He might lose her, but she'd be safe, alive, free, able to go on, and have a life.

He focused on the road, his fingers tightening on the steering wheel as he tried to ignore the rich scent of her natural fragrance swirling around him. Protecting Sarah was worth any sacrifice. He'd give her up if he had to. If she decided she didn't want him after this, he'd let her go.

What happened after that…he couldn't find it in him to care.

CHAPTER THREE

They were on the highway for about ten minutes before Sarah stopped brooding and focused on her surroundings. A sign for Lancaster flashed past.

What the hell? "Where are we going?" she demanded, finally facing Daniel.

She shouldn't have. Looking at him robbed her of reason.

Every single time.

He was a beautiful man—tall with dark brown hair and the most electric blue eyes she'd ever seen. His features were an interesting mix of his Russian father and his Bengali mother, though he bore a much stronger resemblance to his father. Tigers tended to favor the same sexed parent—daughters their mothers, sons their fathers. Daniel was no exception. There were hints of his mother, in the angles of his face and the shape of his eyes, but stood side-by-side, Daniel was every bit his father.

The combination of genes made him one of the most gorgeous men—tiger or human—she'd ever encountered, and she lost her mind every time they were anywhere near each other.

She blinked, trying to banish the breathless obsession. A side effect of her job as a genetics researcher was that she always studied people for their hereditary makeup. But Daniel was another story all together. Her study of him went well beyond a mere interest in his genes.

Her lips still tingled from Daniel's near kiss earlier. Being with him this close to her estrous was so dangerous. Her skin felt hot and tight, her stomach danced in giddy anticipation of his touch. Ignoring his unique scent was impossible in the confines of the truck—that delicious mix of citrus and cumin and flavors with no human words.

After seven Runs, she still couldn't get enough of him. His touch, his taste, the feel of him…They only ever had that time during the Run—at least until she got pregnant—so the weeks in between her cycles made the anticipation stronger.

If she stopped thinking, she knew she'd never be able to keep her hands off him. Even now, with her anger and grief so near the surface, she could lose herself in Daniel.

His hug, his understanding earlier had almost broken her. When he'd pulled her close, all she'd wanted was to sink into his arms and forget the world. The feel of him, hot and hard, strong and solid, was like a balm she couldn't resist.

Then he'd almost kissed her.

For that moment, everything had faded and her entire being focused in on his nearness, his scent, the feel of his breath hot against her lips. Her nerves strung tight with the need to have his hands on her, covering her breasts, stroking her waist, stripping off her jeans. It was all she could do not to pull him into the truck and fuck him until she couldn't think anymore. Daniel would make her forget everything for a few hours.

But then where would they be? He'd still want to keep her from killing Bradley. She'd still be angry and grieving, *needing* revenge like she needed to breathe.

She shook off the dark thoughts to glare at him, waiting for his answer.

He kept his attention on the road as he finally said, "We're going to a friend's house. Somewhere safe." He glanced at her for a second, then faced forward again. "We'll stay there until I'm sure you won't go after Williams again."

"Joseph won't stop." More quietly, to herself, she said, "Even if I could."

Daniel's hearing was superb, even for a tiger, so he didn't miss her comment. "You don't have to do this, Sarah. Let the humans deal with him."

"He killed one of *our* people. How can you let that go?" Fury made her fists clench and her gut tighten. Every muscle contracted with the need to tear and rip and rend Bradley Williams into little pieces. "Su-jin was my best friend," she murmured.

"I know."

Daniel's voice was quiet in the truck's dark cabin, and his soft, caring tone brought her to tears. She returned her gaze out the side window so he wouldn't see the telltale wetness dripping over her cheeks.

She and Su-jin had been friends since childhood. Female tigers were so rare, most who lived in the same country knew each other, at least in passing. But she and Su-jin were close enough in age and had attended the same schools, so they'd had a chance to develop a deeper friendship.

They'd spent all their spare time together, were college roommates, and had traveled through Asia for a year before Sarah started graduate school. They were as close as sisters, closer maybe because Sarah didn't fight with Su-jin nearly as often as she fought with her biological siblings.

She and Su-jin even worked for the same company— Chernikov Research Lab. Sarah was a technician in the genetics wing of the facility. Su-jin was an accountant. They spent most lunches together, gossiping about men, life, their futures, the Mate Run. They debated the benefits and drawbacks of the breeding custom that was saving their species from utter chaos, and questioned whether it was still a viable way to keep mating fair among the tigers. But both had not so secretly looked forward to the Run, the thrill of having the males compete for their attention, and the excitement of letting the man they wanted to be with catch them.

She glanced back at Daniel, as memories of him catching her started that tingling of need low in her belly again. He'd lived up to every hope she had for a mate. Daniel had been clever, cunning, and *fun*, not to mention the sexiest man she'd ever known. Finding ways to try out maneuvering him, leading him through the forest, the thrill of delight and lust when he finally did catch her, every single Run had been a perfect, exciting, erotic joy.

And Su-jin had been so happy for her.

Sarah swiped at her cheeks, not surprised when she couldn't dry the tears with the cursory pass.

Su-jin had been close to starting her own Mate Run. These last few months, she'd been sowing her oats with human men, living a little wild before she settled down to find a tiger mate. Bradley Williams was just supposed to be one of those indulgent flings. He was wealthy, handsome, sexy—if you didn't look at him too closely.

Just the idea that Su-jin had found the man sexy made Sarah gag, knowing now what he really was. Even before she'd understood his true nature, Sarah had been hesitant about him. Some deep instinct whispered a warning. There was something about his scent that rubbed her wrong, though she'd never been able to pinpoint exactly what it was or why it bothered her. It wasn't a *bad* smell. Just…not right.

Now she knew she'd picked up on something in his chemistry pointing toward his psychosis. She'd never come across anything like it before and hadn't known enough to heed her own instincts. Especially since Su-jin wasn't worried. She'd only seen Williams' appeal, and the fact that her father and brother would *hate* him. That by itself made him an ideal candidate for a fling.

Su-jin had been born well after her parents thought they wouldn't be able to have any more children—before Su-jin her mother had only managed to conceive once. Su-jin wasn't a strong tigress either, a weakness she inherited from her late mother. Because of that, her striking resemblance to her mother, and the fact that she'd been born so many years after Joseph, her father and Joseph had coddled and over-protected her to the point that she was desperate for a rebellion.

Sarah took a long, slow, deep breath to choke back a painful sob. Su-jin's innocent need to rebel had gotten her killed. So wrong. So unfair!

And it was all Sarah's fault.

If she hadn't pointed out Williams at the bar, if she *had* admitted Williams gave her the willies, maybe her best friend would still be alive.

Daniel reached out and stroked her shoulder. She shook off his touch. Her skin was too sensitive from a combination of pain and anger, and the fact that her estrous was only a few days away. She couldn't stand his gentleness right now. It made her want to scream.

"Sarah."

His voice brushed her pain. She trembled in the wake of it. "Stop! No understanding. No 'Sarah'. Not now. I need to kill him so badly I can barely think around it, and that's not going away any time soon. You're wasting both our time with this… intervention." She knew her outburst sounded harsh. She pressed her palms against her eyes in a vain attempt to stop the tears still streaming over her cheeks. "Joseph will get to him, even if I don't. Williams is a dead man. Why bother stopping us?"

"Because it will mean a death sentence for you both, damn it!"

His roar echoed in the confines of the truck and startled Sarah so much she jumped. At least it was better than the damned gentle understanding.

She glanced at him. Highway lights flashed in the cab and she saw his knuckles were white, the steering wheel flexing under his grip. He still faced the road, but his expression was dark and hard, his jaw tight.

"Do you think I don't get it?" he said through clenched teeth. "I want him dead, too. We *all* do. Su-jin was one of us and that should never have happened to her."

"Then why are you stopping us?" she hissed. She knew the law. They all did. Kill a human, especially in tiger form, and it was an automatic death sentence. "There have been exceptions in the past. I'm a female. They won't execute me."

"But Joseph won't be so lucky."

"There are extenuating circumstances," she insisted. Her tears had dried and she faced him fully, earnest now. If she could convince him, he might even help her. She picked the most recent example of an exception to the death sentence. "Ivan Chernikov wasn't executed."

"He's the youngest son of quite possibly the most powerful of all the elders. Elizaveta made a bargain for his life that still affects her grandsons more than twenty years later. No cheap bargain. No one will do that for Joseph. And even if they let you live, they will keep you confined for the rest of your life. They don't have a choice. You know better than most that with modern forensics we can't afford to take chances or make any more exceptions."

She wanted to argue, but the stubborn set of his jaw clearly told her she wasn't going to change his mind now. She would though. Or she'd get away from him and finish what she'd started. If she did it before Joseph got to Williams, at least no one would be executed. She'd take full blame and deal with the consequences of a life sentence in her people's version of jail.

First, though, she had to figure out how to get away from Daniel. Or convince him to help her.

As a seeming change of subject, she said, "I heard the fight in the woods—at least I heard Joseph. Who did you bring to stop him?"

His silence told her what she had already guessed.

"Victor will end up helping Joseph kill Williams, you know. They're best friends, as close as I am…was…with Su-jin. Joseph will talk Victor around to letting him kill the bastard."

Daniel shook his head. "Victor doesn't want Joseph put to death." He glanced at her again. "If the roles were reversed, would you let Su-jin do something that earned her a death sentence?"

She faced out the front window, unable to look him in the eye or answer his question. He grunted his satisfaction, knowing what she would do even if she didn't want to admit it aloud.

There was no way she'd allow her best friend to sacrifice herself. But Sarah wasn't going to let her death go unavenged either. Victor might keep Joseph away, and maybe that was for the best. Daniel was right. No one would be able to stop

Joseph's execution if he did kill Williams. If Sarah acted alone, no one else but Williams had to die.

If she wasn't in so much pain over Su-jin's death, she'd have thought of that earlier. Her friend wouldn't thank Sarah for getting her brother killed.

Yes. She had to do this on her own. No backup. Not even Daniel. Because if he helped, he'd suffer the same fate as Joseph.

The thought of Daniel being put to death hurt as much as Su-jin's murder.

Sarah crossed her arms over her chest so Daniel wouldn't see her hands tremble. Though anger and rage pumped through her blood, and revenge was a tangible thing she wanted to grab, spending the hour and a half she had with Williams had robbed her of some of her confidence.

He was insane. A real life psychopath. Su-jin was stronger and faster than a human, but Williams had managed to contain, torture, and kill her. Was Sarah strong enough, fast enough, and angry enough to kill him on her own?

Oh, she was angry enough. No doubt of that. Fury rode her hard and demanded blood. Her tiger roared almost constantly in her head. Containing her animal side was difficult this close to her estrous. She wasn't sure her lifetime of self-control would hold out against her need to destroy.

But the logical part of her—the scientist, the reasonable thinker—wasn't as confident her tiger self could overcome Williams' twisted mind.

She didn't even know *how* he'd managed to contain Su-jin. That one missing fact worried her, now that she was thinking more clearly. It wasn't enough to stop Sarah, but it did give her pause.

"Have they…" She swallowed hard because she didn't want to think about this too closely, but she had to know. "Have our doctors performed an autopsy? Did they find out what he did to…to control her?"

Bile rose in her throat, but she forced herself to face Daniel.

He kept his gaze on the sparse traffic. "Drugged her. Something strong. The coroner says it's similar to a drug called…suxa…suxa—something. I can't remember the name he used. But it's not the same. There's a different chemical makeup to the drug he found in Su-jin."

"What does the original drug do?"

He flicked a quick glance at her, then faced the road again. "It's an anesthetic used to temporarily relax muscles, but it doesn't knock the person out. It's fast acting, mostly used during intubations. The coroner said the drug found in Su-jin's blood was altered, though. Given what she went through physically, the state of her heart, the particular wounds…"

He paused as if not wanting to go into too much detail, a hesitance Sarah was grateful for.

With an audible swallow, he continued, "The coroner suspects she was paralyzed but conscious. He can't be sure what the altered drug does without testing, though, and that's going to take some time. He also thinks Williams made this drug himself because he can't find any records of it being developed."

"Was it made to hold tigers?" she asked. "Does Willams know about us?"

Her heart hammered a little harder. Damn it! She'd gone after him without enough information. If he knew about tigers, if he'd designed a drug specifically for her people, Williams was a more dangerous man than she'd thought.

"The coroner *thinks* the new drug is meant for humans," Daniel cut into her thoughts. "Su-jin seemed to have been given…a lot. If Williams had designed the new drug for our metabolisms, the coroner thinks the dosage would have been smaller. But he needs to do more research. He can't say for sure yet."

"Okay." Shit. She was going to have to be more careful the next time she went after Williams.

"Williams has to suspect something was different about Su-jin," Daniel said, his tone foreboding. "Even if the drug wasn't designed for shapeshifters."

"All the more reason for us to kill him. If he learns about us, if he finds out that drug of his will contain tiger shifters, he's a threat to us all."

"Damn it, Sarah, do you know who his father is? We can't just kill this man without risking everything. Everything! Enough. We won't get revenge directly. We have to leave it up to the human authorities."

"Fuck the human authorities," she growled. "He's still free, even after they questioned him in Su-jin's murder. They won't do anything either because of his father."

Since he'd been in Su-jin's calendar, the police had talked to Williams, but they hadn't even brought him into the station. They'd let him go about his business without pushing for the truth.

Now the human authorities didn't even have a body or any forensics to pursue. Her people had made sure of that by taking everything attached to Su-jin, to protect themselves. They'd even cleared out Su-jin's apartment. The humans had nothing left to work with. All because her people wanted to remain hidden.

Sarah wanted to scream. Protecting themselves meant a killer went free. It wasn't right. It wasn't fair! Su-jin deserved better.

Daniel merged right and took an off-ramped marked with signs for food and gas. Sarah expected him to stop, but instead he drove past the gas station and fast food restaurant, and continued on a narrow road winding through rolling hills and farmlands.

"Where the hell are you taking me?" He'd never actually told her.

"No place you've been before. Don't worry. You're safe with me."

"I'm not worried about you," she snapped.

That was a big lie, but she refused to admit it to him. She didn't even want to admit it to herself. This close to her estrous, she was so very vulnerable to the attraction between them. Especially when she took a deep breath and her head filled with his scent—that combination of unique musk and a tang of citrus and cumin. Daniel's specific *taste* drew her like the heat of a fire on a snowy night.

She studied him from the corner of her eye. Her awareness of him heightened. Her skin tingled and her thighs clenched as her pulse pumped harder. In the faint light from the dashboard, dark shadows danced across his features, cutting them sharper and reminding her of how he looked in the moonlight, staring down at her, intense and intent on her.

Three nights from now, she'd be expected to Run. The part of her that had always wanted Daniel, that reveled in the three days she got to spend with him, rose up from beneath her grief to fill her. Guilt joined the anticipation, but with his heat and scent wrapping around her, the anticipation was its equal.

She looked at him more directly because she couldn't help herself. He glanced her way, his brilliant eyes dark and heated. He didn't hold her gaze for long, but it felt like time stopped and they were the only two people who existed. She felt his look along her skin, tingling down her spine, and her muscles low in her abdomen tightened.

Did he know how conflicted and needy she was? Just how very vulnerable? She wanted him. She always wanted him, and she could smell his desire. But how could she feel such lust when she was still grieving? Her body was like a stranger to her, wanting the man she loved desperately and yet full of pain and hurt and devastation for her loss.

Su-jin would not begrudge her the attraction Sarah felt for Daniel. Su-jin had been their most enthusiastic supporter, always anxious to hear after each Run if they'd managed to get pregnant so they could be together.

Outside of the Run, Sarah and Daniel weren't supposed to be around each other. The realization slowly sunk in. For the first time, Sarah recognized the trouble Daniel could be in just for being with her, for trying to keep her out of danger.

"Does anyone besides Victor know what you're doing?" she asked.

"Alexis. She's with Victor."

"Anyone else?"

Daniel shrugged. "Victor's mother might know. She's looking after their kids until Alexis and Victor can talk sense into Joseph."

"Why are you doing this?" she demanded. "You will get into a lot of trouble if you're caught."

He glared at her for a brief moment. She sucked in a breath. The look in his blue eyes was electric in the darkness. Suddenly, the closed cab filled with the scent of his anger mixing with his desire into a complex perfume that grabbed her tight around the chest.

"How can you ask me that?" he hissed. "How can you think I would stand by and let you sacrifice yourself, sacrifice Joseph's life, maybe get yourself killed by the same psycho who killed your friend? I don't care how angry you two are. This man is not some two-legged deer. Killing him will destroy more than just your lives and I can't allow that. Do you understand? Your life is more important to me than that."

"Why?" she asked again.

For a heartbeat, she saw the hurt in his eyes before he focused on the road again. Then his features moved into a hard, expressionless granite. His fingers flexed around the steering wheel. The sound of the engine seemed loud in the ensuing silence.

She'd hurt him, she realized, but she wasn't sure what she'd said to cause his reaction. Confusion she didn't want to feel and a new layer to her guilt churned in her gut. She shifted positions, putting her back to him as much as her seatbelt would allow, and stared out the side window, watching the barren roadway pass as they moved deeper into the farmlands of Lancaster County.

Damn him anyway. She didn't have time to worry about his feelings. She needed to find a way to get back to Philly. No matter what Daniel said, she still intended to kill Bradley Williams. She would have her revenge, even if it cost her everything.

CHAPTER FOUR

"Mind telling me where this house is?" Sarah asked, again, as Daniel moved the truck off the side road and onto a rural track that wound through a series of horse farms and open fields. A few copses of trees dotted the landscape.

"We're close," he said.

"And your friend?"

"No one you know."

"Human?"

He glanced at her. "Yes. Does that bother you?"

A valid question. At the moment, she hated the entire human race. Their incompetence, their inability to weed out the crazy man, was infuriating.

"Will he be there?" she asked.

"No. She's stationed in Hawaii for the next six months."

"She?" Sarah felt another kind of anger rising. Jealousy bit hard and she cut her gaze to the man she'd spent the last seven estrous cycles with.

"Military nurse. Good egg."

Sarah dropped her chin to her chest and gave him a *look*. His mouth tilted up just a little. She pressed her lips together and turned away. Damn him. He could smell her jealousy. He'd done it on purpose. To distract her, she was sure.

It was working. Suddenly, the question of who this woman was to Daniel nagged at her. She wanted to ask more, to dig into his past with the "nurse", but she didn't want to think about it right now. It would just distract her from her goal. She had to find a way to convince Daniel to let her go. Worrying about his sex life shouldn't be her concern right now.

Still…She knew very little about Daniel's romantic life. They'd never discussed past relationships—only general life stuff, like jobs, family, hobbies, and silly things like favorite movies or places they'd like to travel. But never their human sexual partners.

The idea of going to the home of one of his former human lovers hurt. Sarah tried forcing her mind away from the mysterious nurse, but she couldn't keep from asking, "This nurse a farmer or something?" She gestured to the surrounding pasture lands.

"She inherited a small horse farm from her parents," Daniel said. "She had to sell off their herd because she's still on active duty. But one day she intends to get it going again. Her mom bred excellent show horses."

"Sounds wonderful," Sarah said with a scowl.

Daniel chuckled so she knew he'd heard her sarcasm.

She also knew he was taunting her. Some of her hurt shifted to annoyance. "You can't distract me like this, you know."

"Like what?"

"With jealousy. I don't care how close I am to estrous. This won't work."

He cut her a sideways glance and the sudden heat of it started her heartbeat pounding.

"Jealousy?" he asked. "You should know better than that."

She swallowed. She knew he wanted her. He'd made it clear from the very beginning he intended to win her. But in their world, winning a mate during the Run didn't *have* to translate to a permanent relationship. Commitment, love…those were options not requirements. She and Daniel hadn't actually discussed their future after…if she got pregnant, so while she suspected he wanted more than a baby from her, she didn't actually "know better" where his feelings were concerned.

She'd only met Daniel twice before her first Mate Run. Most females were at least acquainted with the tiger males living near enough to be part of their Run even if they never met them personally. But she'd been introduced to Daniel at the elders' compound in West Virginia when she'd gone to present reports to Elizaveta Chernikova on the research being done at the lab.

Daniel was gorgeous, polite, charming, sexy, and strong. He made her giddy and he showed up more than she cared to admit in her fantasies.

Outside of the two brief meetings, though, they hadn't talked much before she started running. No dating, sex, or romantic associations of any kind were allowed before that, and no contact was allowed between cycles after a female started running. The rules were in place, supposedly, to level the playing field and make the mating process fair for all the males.

In practical terms, most of the females Sarah had talked to knew who they wanted to catch them from the beginning. At least, for that very first time. She'd been no exception. And after three days of the most mind-blowing sex she'd ever experienced, Sarah hadn't wanted anyone but Daniel from then on.

It wasn't just the sex, though. They…fit well together. She wasn't sure how else to put it. They laughed a lot, and played, and talked. Their scents combined to make a delicious mix of flavors unlike anything she'd ever known before. She could be herself with him in a way that had only ever been possible with her family and Su-jin.

There was something deep between Sarah and Daniel, right from the beginning. And seven cycles later, she knew she'd fallen in love with him. But until she got pregnant, they couldn't make their relationship official.

By being with her outside of the Run, he risked everything. Maybe not his life, but certainly his ability to have a life with a mate and children. His chance at a family, a future. *Their* chance at a future together.

A chance she was throwing away for revenge.

If she was locked up for killing Williams, she'd lose Daniel. She'd accepted the punishment she'd face, but in her anger, she hadn't really thought about the fact that she was sacrificing any hope of a future with Daniel, too. Losing him would hurt as much as losing Su-jin had.

What the hell was she doing?

She glanced at him then looked out the window again. Everything in her ached. There was no way to get her revenge and still keep him. Confined, she wouldn't be given a choice of mates. She wouldn't be allowed to marry. They'd let her have babies—through artificial insemination—because they couldn't afford not to. But she'd never have the freedom of a real family life and a husband who loved her.

Yet how could she live with herself if she didn't avenge Su-jin?

Bradley Williams had a lot to answer for, she thought with a bitter knot clogging her throat.

* * *

They reached the farm half an hour later. Neither of them had spoken much in that time and Sarah's nerves were raw from the silence. She jumped out of the truck just to fill her lungs with fresh air and release some of the tension tightening her muscles.

The farm smelled of horses. The scent made her tiger rise with predatory interest. She hadn't eaten much since her friend's body had been found a week ago. She had to eat or she risked her tiger getting the better of her.

"You're hungry," Daniel said.

She frowned. He knew her too well.

"You look pale and thin."

"I'm fine." She should have realized he'd notice. Daniel had always been very observant. "But yes, I'm hungry."

"Bastard didn't even feed you?"

"We were just going into the house when you pulled me out of the car." She waved that away. She didn't want to discuss the details of her fake date. "Are you going to feed me or do I have to go hunting?"

She quickly scanned the surrounding farmland. She'd be taking a big risk by shifting and stalking through the hills in such open countryside.

Daniel's eyes had narrowed when she gazed back at him. She returned his stare, making it perfectly clear she'd follow through on her threat to go hunting.

He broke eye contact first. With a grunt, he motioned toward the front door. "Mary should have something in there to make a meal."

She followed him to the house, taking it in for the first time. It was two stories, small but well-kept, painted a light color she couldn't make out in the dark with a pitched roof. From the outside, the place looked cozy. Homey.

Again, she found herself wondering about this nurse and her relationship with Daniel. Damn the man for bringing her here. Anywhere else and she'd be able to focus on her real goal.

Opening the door, Daniel led her into a small mudroom just off a very large kitchen. The first thing Sarah noticed was how clean the place was—scrubbed and spotless. It still smelled faintly of pine oil and citrus.

"Your nurse is very neat," she commented as she paced the length of the kitchen.

"Yes, she is. Comes with the territory."

Sarah scowled when he didn't correct the "your nurse" part of her comment. Under the clean scent, she caught a whiff of the human who lived here. A tang of soap, female musk and, strangely, pipe tobacco.

"She smokes a pipe?"

"Picked it up from her father, yes."

"That's…unexpected in a nurse."

"We all have vices."

Sarah snorted and started digging through the cabinets. Cans of soup, vegetables, bags of beans, a couple tightly sealed canisters labeled "sugar" and "flour", some sealed packages in silver wrap, unopened bags of crackers, and exactly three boxes of macaroni and cheese sealed in one large plastic bag.

Daniel reached around her and snatched two cans of beef stew. "This okay?"

"It'll do." She wasn't sure how she would stomach food, but stew did sound surprisingly good.

She watched Daniel move around the kitchen as if he knew it well, and that nagging sense of jealousy poked at her again. Rather than give in to it, she settled at the large, wooden kitchen table and flipped through the mail someone had piled neatly in the middle. When she found a magazine on guns, she pulled it from the pile and started turning pages.

Once the soup was ready, Daniel set a steaming bowl before her. "Interested in guns now?"

"Maybe."

"It won't make any difference if you use a gun." He settled across from her. "Guns can be traced. You'll still call attention to yourself. There will be questions, investigations, and a serious chance of our secret being uncovered. The elders won't stand for it."

She tossed the magazine aside, purposefully avoiding his gaze. Damn it. If she could find a way to take her revenge without it calling attention to her people, she'd be able to live with herself and maybe still have a life. But, how?

"Eat," he ordered, distracting her. "I can hear your stomach rumbling."

She pulled the bowl close and spooned up the surprisingly tasty meal. "Little salty," she commented just because she was annoyed.

His mouth turned up in a smile.

The look set her heartbeat to pumping a little faster. A curl of heat settled in her core. She dropped her attention to her soup, focusing on eating. He made it so hard to concentrate. Without doing anything but smiling at her, he captured her full attention. How could he do that when she was still so upset?

Yet, being with Daniel also made her feel…safe. A harbor to escape all the anger and grief. She didn't want to let go of that anger, though. Not while Williams still lived. The internal conflict kept her silent as she ate.

She hit the bottom of the bowl before she realized it. "Was hungry," she muttered, pushing the bowl away.

"There's more."

"No. Thanks." For the first time in a week her stomach wasn't churning with nausea the moment food hit it. She didn't want to risk upsetting the balance.

She hadn't slept much more than she'd eaten since Su-jin's murder either, and the exhaustion weighed on her.

"What time is it?" She glanced around, but the microwave clock blinked a little blue twelve, and there was no sign of another clock in the large room.

"About eleven," Daniel said. "You can sleep in the guest room. I'll show you the way."

"And you?"

"I'll be fine."

"That's not an answer."

He stared at her long enough that she shifted uncomfortably in her seat.

Finally, he said, "I'm finding it hard to believe you've given up on revenge this quickly."

"I haven't."

"Then I won't sleep."

She cursed and stood to pace the kitchen. "You think I'm going to just leave without telling you?"

"Yes."

The fact he didn't even hesitate made it embarrassingly clear he knew her too well. "You can't stay awake forever."

"I can stay awake as long as it takes to talk you out of doing something stupid."

CHAPTER FIVE

Daniel led her upstairs without any further comment. She followed, steaming, wanting to argue more. But after he showed her to the guest bedroom, he left. No "goodnight". No "I'll see you in the morning". No "stop looking for revenge".

Nothing.

Sarah blinked, not entirely sure what had just happened. She'd expected arguing. Even anger. *Something.*

Daniel never just backed off. Not when he had a point to make or an argument to win. They'd spent more than one night in heated debates, though those arguments typically devolved into another round of sex. This was a different type of disagreement, but still. Having him walk away like that was… frustrating.

"What the hell, Daniel?" She called after him.

When it was obvious he wasn't coming back, she gave the room a cursory glance. The pale yellow paint and light wooden floor made the small space bright and open. A double bed with a white wooden headboard had been placed beside a large window, covered with white filmy drapes. A single closet broke up one wall, and a small chest of drawers filled up another. And that was it. Simple, small, but clean and lovely.

She checked the window and confirmed it was locked, but from the inside. She could easily slip out once Daniel fell asleep. A two story drop was nothing to a tiger.

More guilt poked at her conscience, but she pushed it aside. Now that she was thinking more clearly, and Daniel had made the dangers vividly apparent, she knew she needed to get to Williams before Joseph. While she'd rather find a way to kill Williams without it calling attention to her people, she knew she didn't have time to make a better plan. Joseph wouldn't stop, and she didn't want him to be executed. If she killed Williams herself, she would ensure no one else was punished and still get rid of that bastard murderer.

She glanced at the open door, listening intently for Daniel's movements. All was quiet, so quiet she was only aware of his location because she could sense him. He was in the living room.

The guilt tightened in her stomach, uncomfortably churning her still digesting meal. Daniel had always had a solid moral compass. The trait made him an excellent Tracker and was something she admired in him. He wanted her to leave Williams to the humans—even though he understood her need for revenge. Was she wrong to still go after the murderer?

She shook off the doubt. She didn't have time for it. Victor and Alexis would keep Joseph contained for a few days—maybe—but no more. Williams had to die soon, and she had to be the one to do it so Joseph wasn't executed.

She crossed to the bathroom, another neat little room painted yellow. When she was finished using the facilities, she splashed cold water on her face and looked at herself in the mirror. She had circles under her eyes that looked like bruises, and her skin was pale and dry. She wasn't sure how Williams hadn't seen through her makeup. As she stared, she realized she looked… hollow, as if a part of her was missing. She certainly felt that way.

With an irritated grunt, she returned to the bedroom, made up the bed, slipped off her shoes, and laid down without taking her clothes off. She stared at the ceiling, her brain numb. She couldn't even plot anymore. She just wanted to sink into sleep and forget about everything that was wrong in the world. She wanted to pick up a phone and call Su-jin so she could tell her about the argument with Daniel.

Knowing she'd never be able to do that again brought tears to her eyes.

Despite an hour of trying, sleep eluded her. Every time she closed her eyes, she saw Williams' smug, crazy face, or the sweet, open face of her dear friend.

Thoughts of Su-jin led her to remember the autopsy was finished. That meant they'd be laying her friend to rest. Soon.

Sarah sat up, threw her legs over the edge of the bed, and stared into the dark. She had to know when.

"Will there be a funeral?" she asked when she reached the living room.

Daniel sat on the couch, his feet up on the coffee table, his hands behind his head, his eyes closed. He blinked them open in response to her question. She sat across from him in a big, stuffed chair, leaning forward with her arms resting on her knees, too restless to relax.

"They're cremating her tomorrow," he said quietly, "and her ashes will be buried at the elders' compound."

"Joseph won't be there. They'll wait for him."

"Unless Victor and Alexis can talk him down, he's in no shape for a funeral." Daniel stared at her for a moment before asking, "Do you want to go?"

"I should be there."

"But?"

She pressed her lips into a firm line. "I...I don't want to see..."

"It's harder with cremation. Or I should say it's easier to believe they're not really gone."

"Your father?" That was the only person she knew of that he'd lost.

He nodded. "When he died, I had a hard time coming to terms with him not being around anymore. Even after the funeral, I kept expecting him to call or surprise me with a visit, to give me a hard time about getting a mate and giving him grandchildren." He smiled faintly. "I didn't see him before the cremation because I was on assignment, so I found it very difficult accepting he was gone."

"I'm sorry." A band of empathy tightened around her chest. They'd never discussed his father's death before. Daniel always grew distant when she mentioned him so she hadn't wanted to bring up the topic. Now, it seemed important to know. "How did he die?"

"Aneurism. Sudden and unexpected."

"I'm sorry," she said again. Because there was nothing else she could say.

He titled his head in a slight shrug.

"Do you…Does it ever get better? Does the ache go away?" she asked.

"No."

She waited for more, some platitude about time healing all wounds. None came. Oddly, Daniel's simple response filled her with an unexpected peace. Or maybe it was that she could finally relax. She knew he didn't expect her to get over Su-jin's death quickly. He wasn't tossing around bullshit and putting pressure on her to heal immediately like her parents had. He understood. His honesty did more for her grief than anything else had so far.

She pulled in a long, slow breath and leaned back in the chair.

"Do you want me to take you to the funeral?" he asked. "We'll have to leave at dawn to get there in time."

"We can't show up at the elders' compound together."

"We can get around that if you want to go. For the closure."

"It won't help," she stated.

"Probably not, but I'll still take you."

She rolled her head to stare into the cold fireplace. Did she want to go to the funeral? No. Honestly, she didn't. She should. What kind of person didn't want to attend her best friend's funeral? She'd look like an unfeeling, cold asshole if she didn't attend. For appearances sake, she should go. It was the *right* thing to do. But she really, really didn't want to.

"I'm not ready to say goodbye. If anyone asks, I'll just say I was too edgy because of my approaching estrous," she finally said. "That I didn't think I could handle the funeral."

"An honest enough excuse."

He was right. She still felt like a terrible person. Not going to her best friend's funeral had to rank up there as one of the worst things you could do. But if she killed Williams…Would she feel better?

Or worse?

"Go to sleep, Sarah," Daniel said quietly.

"I can't sleep. I'm too wound up."

"Try. I can't stand seeing you so tired."

She looked at him again, really looked, and noticed the signs of stress and exhaustion lining his handsome face. A bittersweet ache filled her. She wanted to crawl into his lap and let him stroke her back until they both fell asleep.

"You're tired, too." She sat forward and set her hands on her knees to stand. "Come to bed—" she said without thinking. Her skin heated. "I mean, you need sleep, too." Because he did.

"I'll stay here on the couch." He held her gaze for a long minute. "It's better if I'm not too close to you right now."

The admission quickened her pulse, and her body was suddenly alive again. She swallowed hard. Being around Daniel overrode her common sense. She desperately wanted to recapture the way they were during the Run, the feeling of the world falling away until only she and Daniel existed.

All she'd have to do was climb onto his lap and kiss him. A kiss, to remind herself there was something good in the world, something hot and important, and freeing. She knew he wouldn't refuse her, as the delicious flavor of his desire spicing his citrus scent filled her nostrils.

After her last cycle, Sarah admitted to Su-jin that she was in love with Daniel. Her friend was so thrilled she'd squealed and lifted Sarah off her feet in a huge hug. The enthusiastic embrace surprised them both. They'd spent the rest of the night laughing, drinking wine, and discussing when and how Sarah should tell Daniel about her feelings.

She'd intended to tell him this estrous—after making him catch her, of course. And maybe after they made love, because after running she usually couldn't wait to have him inside her.

Being around Daniel, letting his musky male scent fill her head and heart…it helped. On a very basic level, having him close soothed her even as it excited her.

As they stared at each other, she could imagine a life with him—children, noise, laughter, sex, fights, and triumphs. A partnership that supported them both through the years.

But to have that life, to see that vision come to be, she'd have to let go of her need for revenge. There was no way to kill

Williams and not lose Daniel, not in the time she had to get to Williams before Joseph did.

Su-jin wouldn't want that for her. Her friend would want her to marry Daniel, have children, live a long time, and love thoroughly.

Yet Su-jin would never have any of those things for herself. She would never know what it was like to fall in love, to have children…She'd never even gotten to Run and experience the thrill of leading all those males on a chase, letting the one she wanted catch her. The release and joy and satisfaction of three days with that man.

Williams had robbed Su-jin of everything. Could Sarah face herself in the mirror if she let that go?

No. No, she couldn't.

Where did that leave her and Daniel?

"I won't try going anywhere," she said. "Not tonight. You'll be able to relax."

He nodded without comment or any change of expression. There was heat in his gaze, but also a kind of unease. He didn't trust her to do as she'd just promised.

A new hurt took another chunk out of her heart. He didn't trust her.

Because she'd given him cause not to.

CHAPTER SIX

Daniel stared at the ceiling until he was sure Sarah was asleep. Even at a distance, he heard when her breathing evened and slowed. He finally relaxed.

With only a few hours until sunrise, he knew he should sleep. He'd hear her if she got up, but the rest would do him good.

He didn't trust her in her current state of mind. That was hard to accept. Until this disaster, he thought he trusted Sarah implicitly. But at the moment, with her still under the weight and pressure of grief, he just couldn't believe she wouldn't try to get away from him.

He scrubbed his hands over his face.

What a mess.

Even if he succeeded in talking sense into her, he still wasn't sure they could recover. He might lose her no matter what happened.

Three nights from now, he had to let her run. For the first time, he worried she might let another male catch her.

When she'd said she didn't care about a lifetime confinement, she might as well have plunged her hand into his chest and pulled out his beating heart. She couldn't have hurt him more if she tried. He was in love with her, not that he'd ever said as much, but she obviously didn't feel the same or she wouldn't be in such a hurry to throw away what they had.

He understood her need for revenge. On a fundamental level, he agreed with her. That was the worst part. If he thought they could get away with it, he'd *help* her kill Williams.

They didn't have that option, though, and he just couldn't see a way to give her want she wanted—what she *needed*. Frustration was a living thing in his gut.

Because he couldn't sleep, he launched up from the couch and went to the kitchen to use the phone.

To his surprise, Alexis answered after two rings.

"How's Joseph doing?" he asked without preamble.

"Bad. I'm not sure this is going to work. He and Victor are signing so furiously at each other, I lost track of the conversation."

Daniel heard a tiger roar in the background.

"Damn it, he's shifted. Again. I'd better go."

"Call when you have an update. You have this number on your phone now?"

"Yeah. Thanks."

Before Daniel could hang up, though, Alexis said, "Wait. I do need to talk to you about something." There was a crash in the background. "Shit. I'll ring you back soon."

The line went dead.

Daniel sighed and set the phone back in its cradle. He sat at the kitchen table and stared out a window into the dark back fields behind the house. Despite their best efforts, they might not be able to save either Joseph or Sarah.

Fuck.

Anxiety woke Daniel from a light doze. To his relief, the sound of Sarah's steady breathing confirmed she was still upstairs and asleep.

Unable to rest more, he went outside into the early morning light and breathed in the clean scent of grass, soil, moisture from a fog hugging the hills, and the faint undertone of horse. He flexed his hands and stretched his arms over his head. He needed a run to burn off his anxiety, anger, and hurt. But he'd picked this location specifically so Sarah wouldn't be able to run around in tiger form easily. It meant he couldn't either.

He supposed he could jog on two legs, but he knew that wouldn't give his tiger the release it needed.

With a sigh, he went back into the kitchen and started breakfast—pulling frozen bacon and sausage from the industrial-sized freezer Mary kept in the laundry room. He also found a sealed container of oats and decided oatmeal sounded good. No eggs, but he knew Sarah hated even the smell of them, and he could take or leave them.

He was halfway through cooking when the phone rang. He snatched it up quickly and then listened a moment to make sure it hadn't woken Sarah.

When he was certain she was still asleep, he said, "Hello?"

"Daniel? Alexis."

"Hey. How's Joseph?"

"We had to drug the idiot. I hate using tiger tranqs, but he didn't leave us any choice."

"Damn. That's bad." The tranquilizers were a last resort for Trackers. They very rarely used them because occasionally a tiger had an allergic reaction, sometimes lethal. It was one thing to kill someone who needed killing. It was another thing entirely to kill them when you were just trying to subdue them. Most Trackers learned other ways to handle unruly offenders, and ways of knocking them out without the drug, though those ways tended to leave marks.

"Fortunately, he's sleeping it off without any trouble," she said. "But he's going to be just as pissed when he wakes up as he was when he went down. Victor's trying not to hurt him, which means Victor's got a few serious wounds that need to heal now."

"And you?"

"Oh, I'm fine. Though it's hard to see it, Joseph does seem to have some sense left in his idiot head, so he's avoided hurting me." She grunted and said, "But since I'm the one who tranqed him, he might not be so hesitant when he wakes up."

"You okay to handle him?"

"Of course." She sounded so offended Daniel laughed.

"Hey, you've been out of the game for ten years now. Training other Trackers isn't the same as practicing your own skills on dangerous prey."

She snorted. "Not a single tiger I couldn't still take."

She spoke with such confidence; Daniel was inclined to believe her. Alexis was a living legend, the only female Tracker in centuries, and good enough at the job to put the fear of death into most reasonable thinking tigers. Those she trained went on to be the most successful, and the scariest, Trackers out hunting. He supposed she'd earned her confidence.

Still, Joseph was a friend. "How much of that tranquilizer do you have?"

"Enough. I hope. Anyway, I didn't call to defend my skills. I wanted to tell you something Victor and I picked up in the woods behind Williams' place."

Daniel straightened, moving the phone to his other ear so he could flip bacon, but his full focus was on Alexis' comment. "Go on."

"When we were intercepting Joseph, I smelled something. Something dead and decaying close to the house. On public land inside the park, I think, but still very close."

"An animal?"

"Human."

"Human?" Daniel's heart rate kicked up.

"I didn't have time to locate it, and I only got a brief scent impression, but it definitely smelled like a rotting human body. Muted, though, like it was buried. And there was some strange, chemical tang, like a drug, but nothing I've ever smelled before. Not like lye to cover the stench."

Daniel frowned and took the bacon off the stove before collapsing into a chair at the table. "Was it a little flowery with some overtones of medicinal cherry, and…well, something that doesn't have human words, but…I don't know, punchy?"

"Yes! That's it."

It was hard to discuss the way their sense of smell translated scents sometimes because there weren't always human words for what they detected. But this scent, he'd caught it once before, and it wasn't something he was likely to forget soon.

"Su-jin had that scent clinging to her when I recovered her body," he said quietly. "The autopsy revealed she'd been drugged. Coroner said the drug is new. He suspects Williams created it."

Alexis was silent for a few beats. Then, "You think we smelled the drug. You think maybe this is someone else Williams killed." She wasn't questioning.

"It's possible, right? He created a drug strong enough he could torture and kill a tiger. What are the odds she was the very first person he used it on?"

"Pretty fucking low," Alexis said. "But would he really have buried the body so close to one of his own houses?"

"Depends on how confident he felt about the body staying hidden."

"He's an arrogant asshole. Cocky his money will keep him safe."

"And he's completely crazy. It's possible he feels invincible."

"Or the body we smelled was his first and he panicked. Or whoever it is can be linked back to him in some way. He didn't bother burying Su-jin after all."

True. He'd left her body in the open, in a ditch beside the highway, nowhere near his own place. Like garbage.

Daniel heard the phone plastic crack and made an effort to relax his grip.

Joseph had already been out looking for his little sister when some human good Samaritan found the body and called the cops. It was a fluke the humans got to her before their people could.

Dumping her in the open hadn't been an accident. It was like Williams was bragging, showing off the results of his handy work. A man who would do that wouldn't stop either. There would be more dead women if the human authorities couldn't prevent it.

That knowledge only increased Daniel's sense of frustration and helplessness.

"You think there's been more?" he asked.

"Hard to say. I couldn't stop to judge how old the body was. I didn't pick up more than one, though. Just that single putrid stench."

But she hadn't been hunting for more. Daniel stared at the wall as he considered an option he hadn't before—what ifs that might actually help. Might…

"I'll check with my police contact in Philly," he said as the possibilities spun through his head. "See if there've been other murders similar to Su-jin's."

"Might get their attention."

"Especially if they find something near a house Williams owns." He heard noise from upstairs and stood, returning to the stove to stir oatmeal and take it off the heat. "Sarah's getting up. I have to go."

"You gonna investigate?"

He smiled. Of course Alexis knew what he was thinking. "Probably. I'll let you know." He kept his response vague because Sarah would be able to hear them now.

"Call me after," Alexis said and disconnected.

By the time Sarah joined him, he had a bowl of oatmeal and a plate piled with bacon and sausage waiting on the table for her.

"Coffee will be ready in a few minutes," he said. He studied her face. Her cheeks were still hollow and there were still faint circles under her eyes. But she didn't look as pale anymore. "How do you feel?"

"Better," she admitted with a slight smile. "I slept surprisingly well."

"Not long, though."

"I've never slept long anyway."

True. At least, during their time together, he hadn't known her to sleep more than a few hours at a time. And when she got up, she made sure he did too, literally. He enjoyed that about her. Waking up to a sexy as hell woman sucking his cock was a pleasure every time. Though the pace she set might wear him out after they were married…

If. If they were married.

The sobering thought was too complicated to consider just yet, so instead he focused on feeding her. She ate well, finishing off every scrap of food and even stealing a piece of bacon from his plate.

"Did you sleep?" she asked.

"A little. Enough."

"Who was on the phone?"

He heard an edge in her tone and wondered what brought it on. "Alexis."

"How's Joseph doing?"

"Not well. They had to tranquilize him."

She frowned. "I told you he wouldn't stop. Is he okay?"

"No allergic reaction. Don't worry. Victor and Alexis are taking care of him."

"Like you're taking care of me."

"Yes."

Tension vibrated between them as they stared at each other. Daniel allowed himself the luxury of her scent, filling his head with her combination of floral flavors with spicy undertones, a complicated mix, powerful and uniquely Sarah.

His gaze dropped to her mouth when she licked her lips. Under her natural scent, he also detected her oncoming estrous. The added tang was like a siren song, calling his lust and need.

He had to keep himself in check. Giving in to his desire now would be disastrous. Not only were they outside the Run, and therefore he risked his future ability to participate in the mating ritual, but if he lost himself in her body and heat, he might forget the point of having her here, the reason he was risking so much.

Would a kiss be so bad, though? Just a little taste. A brief, delicious reminder of what was between them, what they could have if they got out of this mess.

Before he thought better of it, he came around the table and lifted her out of her chair by her shoulders. She didn't resist. He heard her heart beating, saw the pulse in her throat. A warm rush of primal demand and possessiveness filled him as he pulled her body flush to his. Her slight curves fit against him perfectly, like she was designed just for him. When her hands came up to rest on his hips, his muscles tensed, his grip tightened, and he dropped his mouth to hers.

Just a taste, he promised himself. Just a single taste…

The first brush of her full mouth against his destroyed every promise he'd just made.

He angled his head to deepen the kiss. She tasted perfect, sweet and salty from breakfast and that "flavor" that was part of her scent, a rich mix that satisfied and ignited his hunger in equal measure. The brush of her tongue against his was electric, and his hands flexed on her shoulders, pulling her closer.

It would be so easy to pick her up and carry her off to bed. To strip off the tank top and jeans she wore and lose himself in her soft skin and fiery passion. So very, very easy to forget everything and take what his tiger considered *his*.

He slid his hands down her arms, across her waist and down to her ass, pressing her against his growing erection. Her soft moan, the slight grind of her pelvis against his, shot jolts of pleasure up his spine.

The warning buzz in his logical brain was quiet, but persistent. He didn't just want a moment with Sarah. He wanted a life. And giving in here and now, outside the Run, broke rules they couldn't recover from. He'd be banned from attempting to mate for five years. She'd have to choose another male. And that was if she gave up her revenge scheme.

Breaking off the kiss and setting her at arm's length was one of the hardest things he'd ever done. His heartbeat raced as he stared into her dark eyes. She blinked, her breathing coming fast, and he was tempted beyond all reason to drag her close again.

"Not outside the Run," he said, as much to himself as to her.

She swallowed visibly. "There have been exceptions."

"One." Alexis and Victor had been allowed to mate despite breaking the rules of the Run and getting married before Alexis was pregnant. "And ten years later they're still paying off the imposed fine. Things would have been even worse if she hadn't gotten pregnant two cycles after the wedding. And even then there was uproar in the community. If her second baby hadn't been a girl, there was talk of forcing them to separate."

"I hadn't heard that, about separating them." She stepped farther away, as if she finally felt the same worry he did.

He shrugged. "It was a small group of dissenters, and their efforts wouldn't have worked. Alexis and Victor would have fought and stayed together no matter what. They had Elizaveta's backing, too. But they were lucky to have a girl and save themselves the trouble."

The whole community was lucky their middle child was a girl. They needed every single female tiger they could get. Which was the whole point of the Mate Run. It had saved their community when they were on the brink of extinction and threatening to implode from the inside. Without it, the males would go back to fighting death matches over females, even resorting to rape and killing in their desperation for a mate. The rules of the Run were there to protect them all while they tried to find a way to stave off extinction. He believed in the Run and the good it did their people.

But standing in this cozy kitchen, staring at the woman he wanted more than his next meal, his next gulp of air, he had a very hard time remembering the laws he'd spent years upholding. He wanted to break every one of them to have Sarah.

Doing so would make a mockery of the reasons he'd brought her here in the first place, though. To save *her* from breaking a law. How could he tell her not to take revenge, not to break the law that would get her confined, when he was on the edge of doing the same thing? Did it make a difference that the rule he wanted to break didn't involve killing someone?

He thought of Alexis and Victor. They'd broken the rules to be together. But there had been extenuating circumstances, a situation set up to force Alexis' hand. He didn't have that excuse. He didn't have any excuse.

As he stared at Sarah, he acknowledged he was already breaking the law just being with her outside the Run. He had noble reasons for this breech, but if he let things go further, he couldn't claim any kind of moral high ground.

He wanted Sarah for his wife. He would be sacrificing that possibility if he gave in to his need now.

If she'd still have him after this.

"I'm going to take a shower," Sarah said. "Thank you for breakfast."

She left the kitchen at a fast pace, like she was escaping. Though grateful for the distance, he wasn't sure knowing she was naked and wet upstairs would actually help him regain his common sense.

Every breath he took was filled with her and the lingering blend of lust with both their signature scents. Three more days, he told himself as he took care of the dishes. Just three more days till the Run.

Which presented its own set of problems.

He glanced up at the ceiling, listening to the shower water run and trying hard not to visualize Sarah standing in the hot stream. Too easy to imagine walking into the bathroom, stripping off and joining her. Lifting her, fucking her against the shower wall, swallowing the sounds of her pleasure and release…

He shook himself hard and forced his mind to other things while he did the dishes.

Alexis' information about a dead human body near Williams' house opened an option they hadn't had before. There might just be something there to force the human authorities to look closer at Williams, but Daniel wouldn't know until he investigated.

Did he tell Sarah? If they went, if they found a body, they could call the police, tip them off anonymously. Or he could contact Pete directly. Peter Kelly was a homicide detective in Philly, and a contact Daniel had worked with more than once in the past. Pete wouldn't have jurisdiction in Ridley Creek State Park, but he might know someone in the state police who could investigate.

Maybe they could get some sort of justice, even if it was indirect. Would that satisfy Sarah?

He'd be taking a big risk bringing her anywhere near Williams again—even if just one of Williams' properties. The man owned at least five homes that Daniel knew of, and lived most of the time in a townhouse in Philadelphia. But Williams had taken at least two "dates" to the house outside the park, so there was no telling if he'd be there or not. Could Sarah resist the call to kill the man?

Could Daniel?

And would she forgive him if he chose the safe answer and didn't tell her about the body?

He was pretty sure he'd never forgive himself if he didn't do something. He could always try locating the body after the Run. Then again, Williams might move it before then.

Fuck.

Daniel desperately wanted to punch something. He fisted his hands, keeping them safely at his sides as he debated his next move. He hated, hated, hated this. In his world, he was the enforcer. If Williams had been a tiger, he'd have taken great pleasure in killing the man personally. Suppressing his instincts—with both Sarah and Williams—was making his tiger chuff and growl.

He needed to run, to shift and stretch himself, to release the tension, worry, and frustrations dogging him. He couldn't. But he'd never needed a shift so badly in his life.

"Fuck," he muttered aloud.

And made his decision.

They'd go find the body and call it in to the human police. It was something. The only thing he could give Sarah that might come close to satisfying her need for revenge. Then maybe, maybe, when they went into the Mate Run, she'd let him catch her again.

Chapter Seven

Sarah stared at Daniel for a long, quiet moment after he'd finished his story. She'd suspected something when she'd come downstairs this morning—he'd been so vague on the phone with Alexis.

But this…

"Will you be satisfied with the possibility of indirect justice?" he asked. "Can I trust you to come with me?"

Ah, those were the questions. Would this satisfy her? And could he trust her?

The fact that he didn't and had to ask cut deep, but it was an honest concern because at the moment, she didn't even trust herself. She hated that he didn't trust her. She hated more that he had cause.

Given the news he'd just revealed, though, she could worry about repairing the damage she'd done to their relationship later. Right now, she had to decide how to answer his questions.

Could he trust her not to kill Williams if she saw him again?

No. He couldn't. With every fiber of her being, she still wanted to rip out the man's throat.

Would she be satisfied with having him arrested? Harder to answer.

"I still want him dead," she admitted.

"Damn it, Sarah, Su-jin would not want you to throw your life away like this. You can't bring her back, even by killing him."

"You think I don't know that?" She fisted her hands in her lap to keep from launching out of her chair and stalking through the living room. He was right. She *knew* he was right. Nothing would bring her best friend back, and if the roles were reversed, Sarah would never want Su-jin to throw her life away.

"This…his arrest…can give you some kind of peace," Daniel insisted.

"*If* he's arrested." She pointed out the obvious flaw. "Even if the authorities find a body near his house, he's got plenty of reasonable doubt and a lot of expensive lawyers to throw at them. He might not even be taken in for questioning since the body isn't actually *on* his property."

Daniel grunted and turned away. "You're right," he said, then faced her again. "But there's a reason he's buried this body and didn't just…"

When he trailed off, she clenched her jaw to keep in a growl. Didn't just toss the body on a roadside the way he'd done to Su-jin. Sarah's need to kill spiked at the reminder.

"There's something about this body he doesn't want uncovered," Daniel finished.

"We can't dig it up to find out, though, without tainting the evidence. And I don't think we can count on the human authorities to discover the truth either. We should just kill him and be done with it. Bury his body next this other one. That seems fitting."

"He'll be looked for. They'll find him. Sarah." He sighed and stood to pace around the living room.

"I know, I know. I can't help it. I want him gone and nothing short of that will feel completely right."

"You've never killed anyone before. It will hurt you, don't you get it? It will mark you. Even if our laws didn't prohibit it…"

She raised a hand to still his argument. "Right now, how I feel, I would accept that damage to my soul, Daniel. *But*," she emphasized the word when he opened his mouth, "I will deal with that for the time being."

He stopped pacing to face her fully. "Meaning?"

"You can trust me to go with you. I *want* to go." She leaned back in her chair. "I feel like I could kill him, but you're right, I've never killed anything larger than a deer—and that in tiger form. I don't know." She sighed. "I want him dead, but I know Su-jin wouldn't want me to go through with this. It's just so damned hard to let it go. I hate that he gets to walk around free and my friend doesn't."

Daniel approached, but she shook him off. She couldn't take any physical contact in that moment.

"Maybe…" she said, trying to find a way to accept the option Daniel was offering her. "I don't know, maybe we can scent something, a detail we can give to the human authorities along with the location of the body to tie it back to Su-jin's murder. The drug…"

She stopped. The authorities no longer had Su-jin's blood with evidence of the specially designed drug. They wouldn't be able to make the link to Williams being associated with two bodies containing that drug.

"Don't get your hopes up on this ever tying in with Su-jin's murder," Daniel said, echoing her train of thought. "Even if we give them the information about the drug—which will draw suspicion because how would we know about it? —they can't compare it to anything to link the two killings."

"I realized that as I said it out loud. But there might be something else?" She leaned forward in her seat again, settling her forearms on her knees.

He shook his head. "The best we're likely to get, the absolute best, is that the humans link Williams with the buried body. He won't ever be brought to direct justice in Su-jin's murder."

"That's the fucking problem," she grunted.

"Sarah…"

"Yes, I know. I'm trying, Daniel, I really am. This is…a better option than I thought we had. Some form of justice at least. If it works."

Daniel grunted and started pacing again. She couldn't blame him. Restlessness and uncertainty dogged her.

Watching him distracted her from her internal turmoil, and because it was easier than thinking about her situation, she indulged herself. God, she loved the way he moved. He was so gorgeously made, thickly muscled but not too bulky, with long limbs, and a sort of contained grace that reminded her of his tiger form. The jeans and tight blue t-shirt he wore fit him perfectly, too, showing off his yummy body and making her want to strip him bare to see the muscles beneath.

It had taken a great deal of will power not to tempt him upstairs to join her in the shower. Her approaching estrous made her skin more sensitive, and the water was hot and sensual, encouraging rather than dampening her desire. She wanted him so badly, she had trouble sitting still.

All her lustful thoughts continued to fill her with guilt, though. She was still in mourning, damn it. Estrous left her edgy and needy, but she knew she wouldn't feel like this with any random tiger. Only Daniel could distract her like this and take her mind off the revenge she wanted so much.

Daniel finished a circuit of the living room and stopped in front of her, forcing her to straighten to look at him.

"Okay. We'll go. If we get there after midnight, we should be safe enough to search the woods without drawing attention. The park will be closed at that stage, so there shouldn't be anyone else around. If we go in on foot, we shouldn't attract the park police either."

She nodded, eager now he'd agreed to take her.

"But one way or the other, we are out of there before sunrise," he said, his expression stern. "And that's it. No going back and searching more. We find what we can, give the information to the police, and hope they can link the body to Williams. That will be the end of it."

She raised her brows.

"I mean it. No matter what happens, you *have* to give up on revenge. Look what's happening with Joseph? His best friends had to tranquilize him. He's going to end up in confinement. If you can't let go…"

She waited for him to finish, to repeat what he'd been telling her for the last twelve hours. Or tell her that he couldn't take being apart from her, that he loved her. Something to give her a reason to let revenge go. But he didn't finish, he just went back to pacing.

"Could you?" she dared ask. "Could you allow him to get away with killing someone you loved?"

Her question stopped him abruptly. He held very still, and she wondered what he was thinking. When he faced her, his expression was closed and unreadable.

"Rest while you can. Help yourself to more food. Mary won't mind."

She narrowed her eyes. "Won't *she*?"

His expression softened into a faint smile. "There's nothing between Mary and me. Have you picked up a strong smell of me here?"

She pursed her lips and glanced away, embarrassed to answer.

"Sarah. She's just a friend. You'd like her."

She snorted a disbelieving laugh before she could stop herself.

"Was that because she's human? Or because she's my friend?"

She stood. "I need some fresh air." She didn't want to talk about this right now.

Honestly, she was surprised by her level of jealousy. He'd given her no reason to be suspicious. Though, outside of the Run, she had no idea what he did, who he saw. She didn't even know exactly how he felt about her beyond lust. She assumed he cared for her. He wouldn't be doing all this if he didn't. But…Were his feelings enough to keep him faithful between her cycles?

Ridiculous. She found no sign or scent that he spent a lot of time in this house.

Outside of the fact that he knew his way around the kitchen pretty well.

As if reading her thoughts, he said, "I've been here twice since she was deployed to check on the place as a favor for her. Before she left, I'd been inside this house exactly one other time."

"Fine." Her cheeks heated with her embarrassment. She was acting silly. "I believe you." She did, even if her tone didn't make it obvious.

Shit. She really did need some air. "Will you trust me to walk around outside or do you want to come with me?"

"I trust you not to run away now."

Now because he was taking her to find evidence against Williams, she realized. If not for that, he wouldn't have trusted her.

"Do you want company?" he asked more quietly. "Or do you need time alone?"

She needed time alone. "I'd like the company."

He hesitated and then followed her to the mudroom off the kitchen and the door that took them into the open yard.

In the daylight, she could see the property better and spotted the horse barn a few hundred yards from the house. The area was mostly grass and dirt. The house sat atop a small rise, the barn on the same hill. At the base of the hill, a little stream cut through a meadow that was edged by a few trees. Not enough to hide a hunting tiger, but enough to provide shade on a hot summer day.

It was still early enough in the day that the temperature was reasonable, the humidity down. The air currents carried a strong scent of grass. The sun warmed her skin. The place was peaceful. A kind of sanctuary, with the nearest neighbor barely visible in the distance.

Sarah's own retreat was significantly smaller. She made good money, but she'd only been able to afford a little cabin in the woods while still paying rent on her apartment in Philly. The retreat was her territory, the place she went when she needed peace and freedom. She was surprised she felt a similar peace in another woman's territory.

"It's beautiful here," she commented.

Daniel grunted.

She wanted to laugh. Not much of an answer. For a tiger, he'd always seemed so unaware of the beauty of nature surrounding them. Her Mate Run took place in an isolated, hard to reach part of the central Appalachians where they were unlikely to come across any humans. It was beautiful and primal. But Daniel had always seemed oblivious to the scenery.

He'd been fully focused on her.

Her heartbeat jumped and she cut a look at him. In the sunlight, his dark brown hair showed a few lighter highlights. And his eyes…His eyes were stunning, such a surprisingly vivid blue, surrounded by thick, dark lashes.

When he shifted to his tiger form, his eyes stayed blue. That didn't always happen with other tigers. The human appearance didn't predict the tiger shape. But Daniel was a rare white tiger, and he took the stunning color of his eyes into that shape.

He paused when he caught her staring. "Everything okay?"

She nodded, but her throat was dry. Remembering their kiss in the kitchen only increased her need for him. The part of her feeling guilty for her desire seemed to sink farther away, growing dimmer and dimmer as she eased closer to Daniel's heat.

Her nose filled with his unique scent. Delicious. A scent that made her want to bury her face in his neck and just soak him up.

"Sarah?"

She licked her lips. She finally understood why females weren't allowed to be around the males once they started running. Resisting temptation was impossible. She stepped close enough they were touching, her breasts brushing just barely against his hard chest. He was so tall she had to drop her head back to catch his gaze.

To her surprise, he didn't step away. She'd expected him to be strong, to insist on the self-control they needed to exercise. Instead, his chest rose and fell a little faster as his breathing increased. His desire spiked and added an element to his scent that called to her lust. Their scents started mingling. Oh, she loved that smell, the combination of flavors that was theirs, and theirs alone. So perfect and so wonderfully delicious.

He stared down at her without moving to take her in his arms, without dropping his mouth to hers. He was waiting for her, she realized, waiting for her to decide what happened next. The power he gave her was heady and erotic. She could do what she wanted with him, and he'd let her.

He always did.

No one would know if they broke the rules of the Run. No one even knew they were here, except for Alexis and Victor. And they'd hardly say anything. She and Daniel could fuck to their hearts content and no one had to know.

So tempting. So very hard to resist.

CHAPTER EIGHT

Sarah leaned closer, arms at her sides, flattening her breasts against Daniel's chest. If she kissed him, she wouldn't be able to stop, not like earlier. Her emotions were too raw, her need too powerful. The comfort and release she'd find with him would give her a peace she hadn't had since her friend's murder. Sex…no, making love with Daniel would remind her she was still alive. She'd been living with so much sorrow, she craved life.

"No one would know," she murmured, only realizing she'd spoken aloud when she heard her own voice.

"We'd know."

"Do you care?"

"I want you enough, I'd forget to care for the next few hours."

He paused as his gaze darted over her. The look in his eyes quickened her pulse.

Yes, she thought, yes. A few hours of passion. Stolen. Healing. She wet her lips and smiled when he groaned. His chest rose and fell with his hard breathing and the movement rubbed against her breasts, tightening her nipples into tight peeks and sending a spear of desire down to her core. It would be so very easy to give in, to let go, to forget everything but the passion she'd find in his arms.

He was still staring at her lips when he said, "But I would eventually care again, because if anyone does discover this, we'll be forced apart."

She instantly sobered at his words. The fact that he was still concerned about them being separated gave her hope. Maybe she hadn't completely ruined things between them. She'd damaged the trust they'd developed, but if he still wanted her, if he still wanted a future with her, she could repair that damage.

So long as she didn't kill Williams.

She stepped away. "You're right. We can wait a few more days."

At least she hoped they could wait. She hoped three nights from now, when she ran, he'd still want to catch her.

* * *

By the time they returned to the house, she was hungry again. The fact that she was able to eat at all was both surprising and a relief. She knew it had everything to do with being with Daniel. She felt so damned comfortable and safe with him.

"Sit," she ordered when they got back to the kitchen. "I'll make you something this time. You've waited on me enough."

He raised his brows, but did her bidding.

It took her longer to get a meal together than it would have Daniel, but she made the effort. When she set a bowl of tomato soup and a bacon sandwich in front of him, he smiled a relaxed, sexy smile. The one that always made her pulse race. She hadn't seen that smile since the last Run.

They ate in silence and she was reluctant to disrupt the peace. If they spoke, they'd talk about tonight, they'd argue about Williams, they'd have to consider the future. Right now, she wanted to live in this quiet moment and just be. She could imagine a life full of these moments with him. She wanted that life as much as she wanted Williams dead.

And there was the problem. She couldn't have both.

Once they cleaned up after the meal, he broke the silence.

"You should try to rest. We have plenty of time before we have to leave."

She wasn't particularly tired, but he was right. "What will you do?"

"There's a TV. I'm sure there's sports on somewhere." He grinned when she rolled her eyes.

God, she loved him.

"You need to rest, too," she reminded him. She had no idea how much sleep he'd gotten, but she'd bet it wasn't nearly enough.

"I will."

Reluctantly, she went to the bedroom and lay down, not thinking she'd really sleep.

When she woke to a dark room, she had to blink a few times to remember where she was. As she lay there staring at the filmy curtains covering the window, she listened for Daniel. The TV was on, and it sounded like sports of some kind, which made her grin.

Wouldn't it be nice if all they had to do right now was argue over what to watch?

They had something more important to do tonight, though. She still wasn't sure if this would satisfy her. In this quiet farmhouse, it WAS growing more difficult to hold on to her anger and pain. Somewhere during their walk, she'd let go of some of the blinding rage. Enough that the ache of loss dominated the need for justice. But her anger wasn't gone completely. All she had to do was imagine Williams' smug face and the rage returned.

She realized she was in danger of losing herself to her hate. She knew Su-jin wouldn't want that any more than she'd want Sarah to sacrifice her chance at a life with Daniel.

Could she let go? Could she go on without killing the man who'd tortured and murdered her best friend?

Her stomach rolled with nausea.

She'd have her answers after tonight. What they found, what happened after…She would either feel satisfied they'd done enough and move on, or she wouldn't.

The springs squeaked as she hefted herself out of bed. Time to confront her future. And her soul.

* * *

Sarah sat in Daniel's truck with barely contained patience. He'd made her agree to stay put while he doubled back around the house to ensure Williams wasn't here. The only thing keeping her seated was the fact that she wanted to repair some of the damage between her and Daniel.

He'd parked in the same spot he'd used the night before. It was on a relatively empty side road, far enough from the house the car wouldn't be seen or heard, but near enough to make for an easy escape. The road paralleled the park, but was just outside it so they would go in on foot, limiting the attention they might attract from park security.

She realized she was nervously bouncing her leg when the truck actually started vibrating. She stopped, scowling. Another quick glance at the clock on the dashboard confirmed Daniel had only been gone fifteen minutes. Staring at the little blue numbers, she gave him five more minutes and then she was going after him.

Exactly one minute later, he tapped on her window, startling her. How had he managed to sneak up on her? She usually sensed where he was if he was close enough.

She threw the door open and stepped out. "So?"

"No one's at the house."

"He said he had a maid. You're sure she's not there?"

"No cars. The house is dark. No sound of human breathing or heartbeat. She probably doesn't live in the house."

"Great. Let's go." She started to strip, but he put a hand on her arm.

"Let's go on two feet first. We can shift when we get closer to the body."

She frowned.

"The park is mostly empty, since it's closed now, but there are rental cabins inside and some people are camping. This area isn't as isolated as a lot of our retreats. I don't want to risk a random human spotting two tigers stalking through the wood where they don't belong. We can make sure we've got privacy first and then shift."

"Fine."

She blinked as they moved into the woods, letting her eyes adjust to the darkness. Her tiger vision allowed her to see perfectly well, even in the deep shadows under the trees on this moonless night.

Along with her heighten vision, she opened up her most powerful tool, her sense of smell, and allowed all the various night scents to filter through her. There weren't any humans in the immediate area, but she could smell some had been nearby during the day. In the summer, the park was a busy place. Daniel was right, they shouldn't take any risks. Once deep in the shadows, away from paths and roads, they'd be able to hide better as tigers.

They circled Williams' house and entered the park proper before she finally picked up the vague putrid scent.

"Got it," she murmured. "This way."

Daniel allowed her to take the lead, following on near silent feet as they moved toward the stench. It got stronger the closer they got but was still muted by soil and moist leaves. Definitely buried.

"Pinpointing it will be easier in tiger form," she said over her shoulder.

He stilled her with a hand on her arm, and when she turned, he was staring into the distance, his expression intent.

A moment later, he nodded. "We should be safe enough. I'm not picking up anyone moving this way."

She stepped into a small break in the trees and stripped, folding her clothes neatly and tucking them into a high crevice in the branches where no one would see them, even if they were looking. Daniel stepped deeper into the woods opposite the direction she'd gone for his shift. Though she wasn't shy about being nude, around Daniel she was much more aware of her body and his nakedness than she would be with other tigers. Especially right now, with her estrous so close. Not having to see him strip allowed her a measure of self-control she might not have otherwise been able to maintain.

As she let the change take her, she reveled in the feel of muscles stretching and tendons pulling, bones creaking and snapping. She was born to shift, a part of her very being, so while the change did cause a very slight ache, it was a good feeling, like cracking her knuckles or stretching out tight muscles. The result was a kind of release of tension, tension she didn't recognize feeling until she started the process of letting her tiger out.

She wasn't particularly fast at shifting, so by the time she was done, Daniel was waiting for her, his stunning white and black-striped coat practically glowing in the dark. How he managed to do his job when his tiger form was so distinctive, she'd never known. All that white wasn't much of a camouflage away from the snow.

When she joined him, he made a soft chuffing sound, his whiskers twitching as he stood, before moving off toward the stench. As she followed, she realized the combination of white fur and black stripes actually did create a camouflage in the shifting darkness under the trees. She occasionally lost sight of him, but sensed he was there.

During the Run, he'd always seemed to stand out from his surroundings. Even in tiger form, he was like a beacon to her desires. She'd been able to see him clearly and spot him at a distance.

Except, she realized, in those moments right before he caught her. He always managed to surprise her, taking her before she could pinpoint his exact location. Those moments were thrilling, edged with just a hint of fear to add spice to her lust. She adored Daniel chasing her, catching her. But she was starting to realize he hadn't shown her the full complement of his Tracker skills.

When she lost sight of him again, she trotted through the sparse undergrowth to catch up. She found him crouched over a spot of disturbed dirt. The scent of dead flesh was an assault on her nostrils. She knew they'd found the body.

From the look of the ground, churned dirt covered by a layer of dried beech and oak leaves, no new growth covering the spot, she guessed that whatever…whoever…had been buried here hadn't been buried for long. Daniel gently pawed the earth, digging a little furrow, then set his nose closer to the ground. A moment later, he rose and sneezed three times in quick succession, then he batted at his nose with one giant paw.

Now that he was leaning back, the scent carried strongly to her, too. More than just dead flesh. The stench of something chemical with hints of…a scent like cherry cough medicine was the only comparison she could think of, and a few layers of something she didn't have human words for. It wasn't like anything she'd ever come across before.

She stared at the spot, knowing there was a body there, debating what they should do next. They couldn't dig up the spot or they'd compromise whatever evidence might actually be there for the human police. A fact confirmed when Daniel very gently filled in the furrow he'd made and patted the dirt down, brushing a few leaves back over it.

Pacing around the burial spot, she forced herself to absorb every element of the scent, memorizing and analyzing, looking for some detail they could give the authorities that would tie this body to Williams. But with the layers of dirt and the decay, she couldn't filter out anything useful. The chemical was surely the same thing used on Su-jin, but the humans no longer had a sample to make a comparison.

Frustrated, she plunked down on her haunches and stared at Daniel, her tail twitching irritably. He stared back, his blue eyes dark in the low light. This body wasn't enough to get Williams arrested. It was on public lands in a state park. Anyone could have put this body here. Having it discovered near *one* of Williams' homes would hardly be cause to link the body to him.

But maybe it was enough to spark their suspicions after he was questioned in another murder so recently and that body had disappeared. Maybe this one would be enough to keep the humans investigating in the right direction.

She was about to give up and turn back toward the truck when Daniel suddenly shot to his feet, his head high, his ears forward, his entire body tense. A moment later, she heard it too—a car on the driveway up to Williams' house.

They exchanged a look, and then on silent feet, padded back toward the house.

What if Williams had another woman with him? Sarah hadn't considered it until just that moment. What if he had another potential victim? Would Sarah be able to just leave without doing something—even for a human woman?

She held her breath as they reached a dark copse of trees bordering the open area in front of the house.

A car pulled up to the front door, the tires crunching over gravel. Williams' Jaguar.

With only one person inside.

Sarah let out a quiet but audible sigh. Daniel glanced at her, then nudged her shoulder very gently with his. He must have thought of the same possibility.

What would they have done if Williams had brought another victim here? They couldn't just let another woman be tortured and killed. But stopping it would force them to reveal they were here. That would compromise the information they would give the police about the body. Williams could just point a finger in their direction, creating reasonable alternative suspects.

They couldn't afford that kind of attention, or the questions.

She watched Williams climb out of his car and scan his surroundings before going to the car's trunk. Without conscious thought, she crouched lower, not to attack, but to ensure he didn't see her. Daniel went so still she wouldn't have known he was there except that she felt him beside her.

Williams turned from the trunk holding a shovel. Sarah's stomach clenched. She sniffed toward his car, as the horror that he might be here to bury another body made her stomach roll. All she smelled, though, was car wax, leather cleaner, and Williams himself. The shovel even smelled clean, like grass and fresh dirt.

Another wave of relief washed through her. She'd been so set on revenge, and angry at being prevented from getting revenge, the probability Williams might go out and find someone else after she "got away" hadn't occurred to her. What if he already had someone drugged and helpless somewhere? Daniel hadn't scented or heard anyone in the house. Could he have been mistaken?

Oh, god. If she killed Williams, and he did have another victim somewhere who was still alive, there would be no way to save the woman. Sarah would ensure her death as surely as she'd killed Williams.

She wanted to throw up. Daniel was right. She hadn't been thinking. She hadn't seen past her own need for retribution. But this man had killed before. He had a drug he'd used on at least two victims, a drug designed to incapacitate. There was no reason to think the two women they knew about were the only two victims, or that Williams would stop.

Killing him might stop future murders, but it wouldn't save any potential victims he had now. She had no idea, *no idea* what he had done or when. He needed to be handed over to the authorities alive, so he could talk. Just in case…

In tiger form, she couldn't say any of this to Daniel, but he must have felt her shaking beside him, as he gently bumped against her shoulder. She gave him an almost silent chuff but kept her gaze on Williams.

When Williams closed the car trunk, he had something else in his hands besides the shovel. He scanned the area again then he walked toward the trees where she and Daniel hid. Sarah edged backward on silent feet, as fast as she could move without making any noise. Daniel stayed with her. Williams turned into the woods just before reaching them and circled around behind his property, making his way into the park.

Heading toward the burial spot.

Damn it. He was going to move the body.

CHAPTER NINE

Without thinking, Sarah tracked Williams through the trees. They had to see where he moved the body and hope somehow the police could still tie it to him.

Why was he doing this? Had they given themselves away last night? Did he realize they suspected him of murder? Or had he always intended to move the body?

Fuck, fuck, fuck!

Her nose curled as she caught Williams' scent again. The stench of his craziness was so obvious to her now. How had she missed it before? How had she let her best friend get anywhere near this killer?

Guilt was a physical lump in her gut, and that distraction left her careless for a split second. She stepped too hard on some dried leaves and they crunched. She froze as Williams paused and looked over his shoulder, his eyes narrowed.

"Who's there?" he shouted.

She and Daniel remained as still as the trees. She barely breathed as she waited for Williams to move on. After a long, tense moment, he started forward again.

She waited for Daniel to follow. This time, she concentrated on keeping silent. Time for regrets and guilt later. Now she had to focus on doing what she could to point the human authorities in Williams' direction.

When he reached the spot where the body was buried, he set the shovel into the ground and crouched, fingering a place in the dirt. The place Daniel had disturbed.

How the hell could he see that? He was human. She was positive he was. She would have been able to smell "other" on him if he was something more. The tigers were an insular population, but there were things in the world…other shapeshifters, other beings who might have been able to see that disturbed ground. But Williams wasn't one of them. She was sure of it.

Yet, he'd spotted something. In the dark. Without even a flashlight to help.

Damn.

Williams stood and scanned his surroundings again, turning in a slow circle. When he faced them, Sarah realized he'd pulled a gun from somewhere. He held it up and out as he turned, poised to fire.

She held her breath, crouching low.

"I know someone is there," Bradley said, almost pleasantly. "I can feel you watching."

Sarah didn't even twitch her whiskers or swish her tail. She kept everything tucked and quiet. He definitely shouldn't have been able to feel them. Was he just guessing, shooting in the dark, so to speak? Or did his psychosis give him heightened senses?

Williams' gaze narrowed. "Who are you? What do you want?"

Just a hint of agitation leaked into his voice. He was being watched by two deadly predators. Maybe his insanity didn't override common self-preservation instincts after all. He had no way of knowing these particular predators wouldn't actually attack.

Sarah realized Daniel didn't know *she* wouldn't attack. He must be worried about her as they waited. She had no way to relieve his concern except to remain motionless, so she did, trying to let him know she had no intention of killing Williams now.

The man stared at the surrounding trees for a long time before he finally picked up his shovel, but rather than start digging, he considered the point, frowning. He looked into the trees again.

"Ah, ah, ah," he said in a weird sing songy voice. "I'm not that easy."

He hefted the shovel over his shoulder and started back toward his house.

Sarah frowned. So he wasn't going to move the body now? Was that good or bad for them?

He returned the shovel to his car trunk and then went into his house while Daniel and Sarah remained safely hidden in the trees.

Now what? If they left to call the cops, they gave Williams time to move the body unobserved. If they remained, they wasted time. If they separated…As far as Daniel was concerned, if they separated, he risked her trying to get her revenge.

They needed to shift so they could talk.

She nudged his shoulder and motioned him away from the house. She led him to the place where they'd left their clothes and changed back to human form. She dressed while Daniel shifted, keeping her back to him so she wouldn't have to see him naked.

When she was sure he was ready, she faced him. "Now what?" She spoke in a whisper too quiet for a human to hear, because even though they were a ways from Williams' house, she didn't want to take any chances. Not when he was proving to have better senses than a human should.

Daniel stared at her. "We need to contact the human authorities and try getting them here tonight, before he has time to move the body. They might have cause to search his car and find that shovel."

"Why? The body isn't on his land. They have no legal reason to suspect him. Besides the shovel smells like grass and dirt, *not* dead body. It's not going to have evidence on it."

"But it's suspicious. A shovel in the back of a Jag? It's something. The person who's buried probably has friends and relatives who might be able to connect Williams to the body. That could give the cops cause to search his property."

"They won't get that information fast enough to keep him from covering up evidence. And what if he moves the body while we're gone?"

"Then we'll just have to—"

Daniel stopped short and his head came up, his gaze narrowing. A beat later, she heard what had caught his attention. The house door opening and closing.

"He's leaving?" she mouthed.

Daniel shook his head and continued listening. She focused on the distant sounds too, waiting for the car to start. It didn't. Instead, she heard…nothing. They were far enough away that she wouldn't be able to hear Williams breathing, but she should be able to hear him walking. Maybe he was just standing outside his door? Maybe he hadn't actually come outside and just opened the door to…put trash out or something harmless.

But as Daniel continued holding himself still and watchful, anxiety crawled through her gut. Then she heard it, a snap of a twig.

"He's coming this way," Daniel said in a hushed tone. He grabbed her arm and dragged her deeper into the trees, back toward the park.

"He can't know we're here," she said.

"He suspects something, though. Take a deep breath."

She did and realized what Daniel was talking about. Gun oil—not the same smell as the small pistol he'd held up earlier. "He's got another gun?"

"Yes."

"A bigger gun?"

"Can't say. Just don't want you anywhere near it."

"We need to get to the truck."

"He's angling across that direction, cutting us off. He's closer to the truck than I like. We risk being seen if we try passing him."

"We can move fast enough…"

"You saw him spot the place in the ground I disturbed. Don't assume anything with this man. Even if all he sees is the truck and a license plate, we'll be fucked. We can't risk going directly back. We need to lead him away, then make a wide circle back."

"Shouldn't we shift then? If he sees us in human form, we're in trouble, too."

"And if he sees tigers where they don't belong?"

"He'll recognize us both like this, though. If he tells people he saw tigers, no one will believe him."

"Good point. Especially since the ground is dry enough, we aren't leaving discernible paw prints. Okay." He raised his head, as if gauging his location. "This way, as fast and quiet as you can. We'll put some distance between us and him and then shift."

Daniel took them deeper into the park. She clearly heard Williams now that he was inside the woods. He was extremely quiet for a human, moving like a skilled hunter, which was more than a little unnerving. But her sensitive ears still picked up enough to allow her to pinpoint his location.

How the hell had they become the hunted instead of the hunters?

To avoid making noise, they didn't jog nearly as fast as they were able, but it was enough to give them the brief window they needed.

Stripping quickly, she glanced around. "Where do we leave the clothes and shoes?"

"Tie everything up in a bundle. We'll carry them. If he or the authorities find our clothes, they could lead them back to us."

"We need to get to a phone." This was one of the rare times she regretted never getting a cell phone.

"I know," Daniel said. "We will. Just not with Williams on our tails."

Despite the tension, Sarah's heart beat faster when Daniel took off his jeans and t-shirt. A part of her, the part that wasn't worried about being shot by a crazy human, got a little charge out of this adventure.

As she let the tiger take her, her excitement started outweighing her anxiety. Her tiger recognized danger, but also viewed its own skills as superior. As she rose up on four paws, she savored leading the human on a wild-goose chase.

Digging her claws into the dirt, she stretched her long muscles. Then picked up her bundle of clothes in her teeth and faced Daniel where he stood waiting for her. They took off at a fast lope, purposefully drawing Williams after them.

The run through the dark woods was far more freeing than the situation should have allowed. She let her body move on instinct and savored the stretch and pull of thick muscles and heavy limbs. Letting this part of her out released days of tension and frustration. She needed this.

Her ears twitched as she listened for Bradley. He'd changed directions, picking them up and tracking them.

Daniel led her deeper into the woods, keeping well away from any hint of human presence. This area was relatively isolated. Williams had likely chosen a house at this edge of the park for that very reason. This was as quiet and isolated as he could get and still be close to Philadelphia.

She and Daniel paused at the edge of a sluggish stream. Daniel raised his head, staring back toward their "hunter". Rather than jumping over the stream, he switched directions, keeping Williams close.

As they drew him in, Sarah suddenly realized she couldn't hear him anymore. She'd been following Daniel and lost track of Williams' location. When Daniel stopped abruptly, his head up and moving as he scented the air, she realized he'd lost Williams, too.

The man must have stopped moving. He was quiet, a good hunter, but not quiet enough when walking to avoid their sensitive hearing. He was down wind too, because she couldn't smell him at all. She and Daniel both faced the direction they last sensed him and waited, crouched low, listening intently.

The fur on her nap rose as instinct warned her all was not well. She eased back to put a tree between her and the area she thought Williams might be. Daniel did the same, but because the human was no longer moving, his exact location was impossible to detect.

If he'd been a tiger, they would have sensed his location. She wasn't able to do that with humans. Daniel might be able to but as far as Sarah knew, most tigers could only locate humans by sound and smell.

They waited, muscles bunched and ready to move, still as was physically possible. She let her belly touch the soft, dry dirt but remained ready to spring up if necessary. She searched with her eyes as well as her ears, looking for any telltale glint off Williams' gun, or even the flash of light in his eyes. Her eyesight was far superior to a human's in the dark, but if Williams was a hunter, he would know how to keep from giving himself away visually.

Tension vibrated through her muscles and her heart pounded. She considered moving closer to Daniel but didn't want to risk calling attention to their location. The longer they waited, though, the closer dawn drew and the harder it would be for them to get out of the area without being spotted. On the other hand, Williams would hardly risk digging up a body once it was light, so the closer they got to dawn, the better chance they had of getting the human authorities here before it was too late.

Frustrated that she couldn't say all this to Daniel, she adjusted her position just a little, angling ever so slightly closer to him. Without taking his gaze off the trees ahead of them, Daniel moved a few inches closer to her.

She saw the flash of a rifle blast seconds before she heard the sound of the shot. A blink later, to her horror, Daniel was in front of her and she heard the bullet thud into him. The smell of blood and hot metal washed over her as Daniel dropped to his side.

She roared in denial, dropping her bundle of clothes. The sound echoed off the trees, shocking even her after the almost perfect silence. Another bullet thumped into the tree she'd been crouched behind, hitting where her head had been only moments before. They had to get out of there.

She grasped the thick skin and fur covering the back of Daniel's neck in her mouth and dragged his heavy body deeper into the trees, faster than a real tiger would have been able to move.

The rifle shot had given her a good idea of where Williams was, but she wanted to be out of range faster than he could catch up. When she felt she was a safe distance, she dropped her hold on Daniel and nudged around him, looking for the wound. A thick band of red ran down his shoulder. The bullet was still in there, but had hit him in a non-fatal location, thankfully. A wave of relief left her nauseous.

She had to get Daniel help, to get the bullet out. His tiger healing would take care of the rest. Already, the blood flow was slowing. But with a bullet still inside him, even if the wound healed over, they'd have to open it up again to get it out.

Shit.

She raised her head and tested the wind, angling her ears to pick up Williams' location. He was working his way toward them. She nudged Daniel. His low, quiet burble, almost but not quite the sound of a domestic cat's purr, washed a sense of relief through her. She nudged again. If he couldn't walk, they were in trouble. She could drag him, maybe even carry him back to the truck if needs be, but not while Williams was still hunting them. She'd move too slowly with the weight of a full grown male tiger in tow. And dragging him had surely left a trail. One Williams might be looking for even now.

To her relief, Daniel slowly rolled up to his feet. He couldn't run, his front left leg barely took his weight, but at least he could move.

She jutted her head back in the direction of the truck. The problem with that way, though, was that Williams was still between them and the vehicle. They hadn't gotten enough space to circle safely around him yet.

Daniel shook his head and nodded deeper into the woods.

Oh, no. He was in no shape for that. Lightly, she gripped his neck in her mouth, then nodded at a wide angle to circle around Williams back out of the woods. She saw the consideration in his deep blue eyes, watched him weighing up their options. And she knew the idiot would try protecting her, just like he had by jumping in front of that bullet.

Well, she was having none of it. She forced his hand by moving the direction she wanted to go, knowing he'd follow rather than let her get too far away. This time, she closely tracked Williams. As they moved, the wind shifted and she finally caught his scent. Ah, that was better. She pinpointed his location easily, even though he'd stopped moving again and she couldn't hear him.

She stalked silently, slowly, taking her time and giving Daniel plenty of room to keep up. Williams was still trying to locate them. He had to suspect he'd wounded…something. Had he seen them? Or was he shooting at a flash of color, a flicker of light in their eyes, something hinting where they were but didn't actually allow him to see what he was shooting at?

She'd roared. Williams would know he was tracking animals now. If he was a hunter, he might even recognize the sound as tiger. She wasn't sure if that made the situation better or worse. But there was nothing she could do about it now. Not while Daniel was injured. Not when they still had a lot of ground to cover.

When Williams moved again, he continued heading in the direction they'd been. Sarah flicked her ears back and forth. He'd lost track of them and didn't realize they were circling around him. That would have been a relief if he were any other human, but she didn't trust him to give up or lose them so easily.

The journey to the truck was a tense, slow, painful progression. They were halfway there when she caught the sounds of Williams moving toward them again. He was a ways away, but no longer moving in the wrong direction.

Their lead was sufficient enough that they reached the truck with time for her to shift. She and Daniel had both dropped their clothes in the place where he'd been shot, a mistake that might come back to bite them in the ass later. Evidence of human presence, the possibility the clothes could somehow be traced to her and Daniel, was disastrous. But she didn't have time to go back and recover the clothing.

As she forced her tiger down and retook her human form in a snap of bone and stretch of muscles and tendons, she realized they had a few more problems.

She would be driving nude. With a wounded white tiger in the front of the truck. And if they went to any of their people's doctors, Daniel would get banned from the Run for being with her. Yet, she couldn't go to a human doctor. Or even a human vet. Daniel would heal too fast, especially once the bullet was removed. They'd risk exposure—the very thing they were trying to prevent with all this subterfuge.

What a fucking mess.

Guilt caught in her throat as she opened the truck for Daniel to jump into the passenger seat. He didn't dare shift until they removed the bullet for fear of complications. But he was too big to be inconspicuous. Especially sitting next to a naked woman. She rounded the truck to the driver's side and then poked around in the small area behind the bench seat. Ah, Daniel, you genius, she thought with a grin. He had a change of clothes stored there. Smart, smart tiger.

The sweatpants were huge on her, large enough to cover her completely all on their own. She slipped into the huge sweatshirt, then climbed behind the wheel.

The clothes smelled of Daniel, overwhelming her with a combination of peace and anxiety.

She opened the ashtray and snapped up the keys Daniel had left there when he'd first gone to check out Williams' house.

"Don't worry," she said aloud, putting the truck into drive. "I'll get you help."

He grunted and settled his head on the bench next to her hip, his nose nearly butting her. She reached down without looking at him and ran her fingers through his thick fur, clenching and releasing the softness covering his neck.

She left the truck lights off and slowly eased the vehicle to the main road, cracking the window so she could catch Williams' scent if he got close. When she'd slipped the sweatshirt on, she knew he was still far enough away that he'd have to run to reach them, and even then, he wasn't likely to see more than just a dark colored truck. At least, she hoped so.

She checked the rearview mirror again.

Then she heard Williams' car starting up in the distance and her pulse jumped. Shit. If she didn't hurry, he'd catch them before they could get to the main road or anywhere near the highway.

Tossing caution to the wind, she put her foot down and sent the truck careening down the street, bumping along in a way she knew was uncomfortable for Daniel.

"Sorry," she said.

Daniel just grunted and adjusted his position on the floor. He was so large, he couldn't fit on the bench next to her without his head hitting the roof and was too long to stretch out beside her. His butt on the floor and his upper body on the bench couldn't be a pleasant way to ride, but it was better than the truck's bed.

She reached back and pulled the seatbelt across, clicking it into place. She was sitting at the edge of the bench because she couldn't adjust the bench forward without crowding Daniel, so she wasn't sure the seatbelt would help at all, but it was something to keep her stabilized as she forced the truck to accelerate.

The wheels spun as she fishtailed onto the main road leading toward the highway. She gunned the poor truck again, pushing it to move as fast as it would go. She still heard Williams' car behind them. His Jag was a whole hell of a lot faster than the truck. He'd catch them if they couldn't reach the highway soon and lose themselves in traffic.

She glanced at the dash. Four am. Wasn't going to be much traffic outside semi-trucks, but it was something.

She ran red lights and blared past the two cars she encountered, but she wasn't fast enough. In the rearview mirror, she spotted the Jag's headlights catching up. Fuck, that car was fast. She realized her own headlights were still off, though, which meant unless she hit the brakes, he'd have a hard time seeing the truck even under the streetlamps. So she kept the lights off until just before hitting the highway on ramp, then flicked them on and raced onto a mostly empty road, her pulse pounding.

A fleet of semi-trucks appeared ahead, at least five of them traveling close enough to give her cover. She raced toward them, continuously checking the mirror. Williams' Jag hit the highway just as she moved in front of the rear truck.

She wasn't sure if he'd seen her or not, but she did know he'd catch up with them on the smooth road without other traffic to complicate things.

As she was considering her options, the trucks around her all suddenly slowed. She had to break hard to keep from slamming into the back of the one in front of her. Daniel grunted at the sudden change of momentum.

Panic started her trembling. What the hell was happening? Why were they…?

Then she spotted the speed trap. And a moment later, she heard the sound of sirens on the road behind them.

Changing lanes so she could see behind the barrier of the trucks, she caught sight of Williams' car being pulled over. She laughed. Then hooted, "Thank you, highway patrol!"

She never thought she'd be so grateful for human authorities. She was sure Williams wouldn't give them reason to check his trunk. But sunrise was only an hour away. This would slow him down. Chances were good he wouldn't be able to get back and move the body until nightfall. That gave them time to point the authorities toward that burial spot.

And hope for the best.

She shook off the sense of relief and triumph when she considered the predicament she still faced. Daniel needed help. He wasn't going to bleed to death, but he was in pain and that bullet would continue to cause problems until it was removed. They needed a doctor, preferably a surgeon…

The answer was one she was sure Daniel would hate. Especially since, technically, Ryan was still a medical student. Her younger brother was years away from his residency. But he was a genius. He'd be able to help.

She hoped.

Chapter Ten

The sun was up by the time she parked the truck behind her brother's apartment building. She turned off the ignition and momentarily watched people starting to move around, getting their day started. Then she said to Daniel, "Wait here. Try staying out of sight."

He blinked slowly at her, a look that wasn't hard for her to interpret.

"Yes, I know you're too big to hide. But…try?"

He settled his head on the seat and closed his eyes. She frowned.

"You're not going to pass out are you?"

He opened his eyes and shook his head, then settled back down, closing his eyes again.

Worry gnawed at her gut as she hurried to her brother's door. His car was still in the lot, so she hoped he was home. Ryan was spending the summer in Philly, doing an internship at the lab where she worked. Their parents insisted he support himself between semesters. She'd had no way of knowing that by getting him a job, he'd be close enough to help her with Daniel.

He opened the door dressed only in a pair of pajama bottoms, his messy black hair hung like a mop above his handsome face.

His eyes narrowed when he saw her. "Sarah. What are you doing here?"

"Why aren't you dressed for work?"

"It's only six a.m. And I have the day off. What the *hell* are you wearing? You raid the men's department?" He smirked and leaned against the door jam, crossing his arms over his chest.

"I need your help." Her serious tone made him straighten. "And I need your…discretion. Okay, I need you to keep a secret. From *everyone*. I mean everyone."

"Mom can ferret out secrets."

"You have to keep this one even from mom. Promise me."

"What's going on?"

"Promise first."

"Fine, fine, I promise. What's the problem?"

"I have Daniel in a truck out back. He's been shot. The bullet's still in his shoulder."

His dark eyes narrowed to slits. "You have a lot to explain."

"Later. We need to get him inside. And I need you to remove the bullet."

He gaped at her. "I'm not a doctor yet."

"You know what to do?"

"Yes. Theoretically. I've never performed surgery before though."

The last was filled with sarcasm. She shook her head. "It doesn't matter. He'll heal. We just have to get the bullet out. Do you have a sharp enough knife?"

"I have a scalpel set mom and dad got me for my birthday."

"They bought you scalpels?"

"Can we discuss their horrendous gift-giving skills later? There's still the big problem of getting Daniel inside. Is he…?"

He looked around as he trailed off and she realized his neighbors could appear at any moment. Quietly enough only he would hear, she said, "He's tiger."

"Oh, good. That makes it so much easier." With a sigh, he said, "Wait a sec while I get something on." As he moved back into his apartment, she heard him grumbling, "How the hell are we gonna get a tiger inside without being seen?"

She studied the hallway. If they could get Daniel from the truck, through the back door, and into the building, they stood a decent chance of getting him inside before any of the neighbors caught them. The hall was extremely quiet. She heard a TV set at the far end and some movement in a few of the nearer apartments, but hopefully it was still too early for them to start leaving.

When her brother rejoined her, he had on a t-shirt, jeans and slip-on tennis shoes. He glanced down at her bare feet. "Not too obvious."

"I'll explain later. Let's just get Daniel inside. He can't stay hidden for long."

"Where is he in the truck? Backseat? Cabin? Flatbed?"

"Cabin."

"Maybe anyone passing will think he's one of those giant stuffed animals."

She punched her brother's arm, none too gently, and followed him into the elevator down to the parking lot.

They searched the lot as they moved to the truck, Sarah scenting the air. So far so good. Tension bunched her muscles as she opened the driver's side door. Daniel raised his head just enough to spot Ryan, his eyes narrowing.

"Best you're gonna get," Ryan said. "Seeing as how you happen to be with my sister outside the Run, I wouldn't go casting aspersions."

Daniel flopped his head back onto the seat for a beat, then very slowly climbed up onto the bench, crouching with his paws under him, prepared to leap from the truck. They checked the lot again.

"Okay, wait," Ryan said. "I'll go open the door. Get inside as fast as you can. Your injury slow you down?"

"Yes. He can't move anywhere near as fast as normal," she answered for Daniel.

"Just…As fast as you can. Wait till I get the door."

Ryan trotted back, opened the metal door, then motioned them forward. Sarah nodded to Daniel and stepped back so he could jump to the ground and pad on silent feet to the building. She took up the rear after closing the truck and hurried into the cool dark interior at a rush. The hairs on her arms and nape lifted as tension made her pulse race. She hadn't noticed anyone, hadn't even felt that telltale tingling along her skin when she was being watched. With luck, they'd been unobserved.

Their luck held all the way back to Ryan's apartment. When he closed and locked the door behind her, she dropped back against the wall and released a long, loud sigh.

"Don't relax yet," Ryan said. "I still have to jump years ahead of my current experience level."

"You can do it," she said with confidence.

He tilted his head. "You're not just saying that, are you?"

"Of course not. I trust you to take care of Daniel."

"Well, hell. Guess I have to now."

She grinned, then hurried after the man she loved, finding him settling onto Ryan's charity store couch. He turned his wounded shoulder up, ready for inspection.

Ryan gave the wound a quick look, poking around Daniel's fur at the edges of the injury without actually touching the bullet hole. A pinkish red covered half of his shoulder and leg, but the wound itself had stopped bleeding and was already starting to close.

"Gonna have to cut it back open," Ryan told Daniel with a hint of regret in his otherwise clinical tone. "I don't have any kind of drugs to help stave off the pain. Can you take it? Or do you want me to go out and find something we can use?"

Daniel shook his head and flicked his shoulder in Ryan's direction, then lay back against the couch, relaxed and ready.

"I guess that means we get this over with now." Ryan rose and disappeared into his room.

Sarah knelt beside Daniel and stroked his fur-covered cheek. "I'm sorry," she murmured. The fact he couldn't answer back made this easier. But since her brother could hear them, she kept her words vague. "I'm sorry you were dragged into this. And that you were hurt."

He grunted, a noise that sounded irritated. They had a lot to talk about when he could shift back to human.

Ryan returned with towels, rubbing alcohol, a box of latex gloves, a roll of bandage tape, some gauze pads and a leather wrapped bundle. He set everything on the coffee table, then disappeared into the kitchen, returning this time with a bowl full of hot water.

He motioned Sarah aside, then took up a place next to Daniel, staring at the wound as he moved towels to the floor under the couch. "Can you lift up?" he asked Daniel, who complied so Ryan could move towels underneath his upper body.

"Sorry about your couch," Sarah said.

"You don't want to know what's happened on this couch," Ryan said.

Sarah glared. But he was right. There were some things a sister did *not* need to know about her brother.

Ryan unwrapped the leather bundle and laid it out flat, revealing a series of surgical tools, all shiny and chrome. Sarah recognized a couple of the scalpels, but the rest were a mystery.

"Nice," she commented.

Ryan just grunted. He pulled out two gloves and slipped them on, then selected a scalpel. As he worked, he said, "I'm not going to try stitching the wound. Even after I cut this open again, it'll heal fast enough to prevent infection. I'll bandage it just to keep it neat until the skin closes over."

He raised the alcohol and winced. "Sorry, this is going to sting, but I want to make sure the area is sterilized as much as possible."

He used one of the gauze pads he doused with rubbing alcohol to pat the area around the bullet hole. Daniel tensed and then relaxed. Sarah's stomach turned.

As Ryan set the sharp point of the knife against Daniel's skin, Sarah's nausea rose and black spots danced at the edge of her vision. Afraid she might pass out, she turned her back on her brother's work but knelt down near Daniel's back legs and set her hand on his hip, trying to comfort even though she couldn't watch the procedure.

Daniel's muscles bunched under her touch, tense and hard. Ryan murmured a running commentary of what he was doing—which didn't help Sarah much, but it was better than watching.

Unfortunately, she heard everything too clearly. The sucking sound as Ryan extracted the bullet made her gag. She buried her fingers in Daniel's thick fur and tried concentrating on the warm feel of him, the scent of his natural musk underneath the metallic smell of blood, the steady sound of his heartbeat.

"You can look now," Ryan said after a few minutes.

She released a low breath and closed her eyes, letting her body relax. Daniel's body relaxed too, his muscles easing under her palm.

When she opened her eyes, she saw Daniel staring down the length of his body at her. She smiled weakly, then looked at the work her brother had done. The area around the wound was clean now, most of the blood washed out of Daniel's fur. A clean white bandage was set against the wound, the tape wound around the top of his leg.

"You need to rest," Ryan said to Daniel as he cleaned his tools and put them away. "You can probably shift back now, but I'd recommend waiting another hour, until the wound has closed up. It's deep enough, if you shift, it'll remain open. If you wait, the shift should heal it completely. Won't even know it was there."

He looked up at Sarah and blew out a breath, his eyes wide. "I can't believe I just did that."

She grinned. "I had no doubts."

"You almost passed out, though, didn't you?" He smirked.

"Did not." But she couldn't meet his gaze.

He chuckled as he gathered up his tools. "You want to stay on the couch?" he asked as he stood. "Or you can take the bed. You need sleep. Even though you handled that well, your body won't be happy to have gone through surgery without drugs. You'll heal quicker if you sleep."

Daniel let out the tiger equivalent of a sigh and stayed where he was.

"Couch it is, then." Ryan returned to the bedroom with all his gear.

When he was out of the room, Sarah murmured, "I have to leave to make the call. I've waited too long as it is."

Daniel nodded. Then shook his head, his big eyes narrowing.

"I'll come back when I'm done. I'm going to use a payphone so it can't be traced. And if I wait any longer, the chances of…"

She glanced toward the bedroom, then said, "I want everything in place."

Daniel chuffed and started getting up.

"Oh no you don't," she said, putting a hand on him. "You heard Ryan. You need rest. Sleep. I won't be long. You're safe enough. There's no way—and no reason for that matter—for *him* to come here." She paused when Daniel jerked his head in her direction. "I gave him a false last name and occupation, and I met him at a neutral location for our 'date'. He doesn't know where I live, or have my real name to track me. Besides, Ryan uses our father's last name and I use our mother's. He has no way to find us here, even if he wanted to."

Daniel still lifted up so he was lying on his stomach instead of his side and he held her gaze.

It took her a moment to realize why he still objected. Then she remembered she hadn't had time to discuss her epiphany with him.

"I'm not going after him," she whispered, close to Daniel's head in hopes her brother wouldn't hear. "I can't discuss it now, but I realized in the woods, he was better off alive than dead." Even quieter, she said, "If there are…others, still alive…"

He pulled back and blinked at her. He wrinkled his nose and his ears twitched. After a moment, he thumped his tail twice against the couch. Then he shifted back onto his side and relaxed.

Sarah smiled. She wasn't sure if he trusted her again, but he was willing to take a chance that she was telling him the truth.

Chapter Eleven

Ryan came out of his room as Sarah stood to leave. "Who's *him*?" he asked.

"No one."

"Have anything to do with why you're with Daniel outside the Run?"

"Don't push, little brother. I mean it."

"You do realize you have to be at the Run site tomorrow night? A lot of males are gonna be really pissed off if you don't make it."

"That won't be a problem. I have an errand to do now. Then I'll make my way down."

Ryan glanced at Daniel. "You still running?"

Daniel growled, low in his throat, a warning Sarah couldn't interpret.

Ryan seemed to understand, though, because he raised his hands. "Okay, man, no reason to get grumpy. You'll be ready. Just don't get shot again between now and then."

Daniel grunted and laid his head back on the couch.

Sarah hurried to the door. "Where's the nearest payphone?"

"I've got a phone," Ryan said, following her.

"Need a public phone."

He narrowed his eyes. "There's one outside the convenience store a block away. You know the place?"

She paused with her hand on the doorknob, remembering she didn't have any money on her. Or any shoes. "Can I borrow some change? And a pair of shoes?"

Her brother rolled his eyes and returned to his bedroom, coming back with a handful of quarters, a twenty dollar bill, and a ratty pair of tennis shoes that were two sizes too big for her.

When he handed her the twenty, he said, "In case you need more change."

"Thanks."

"If you don't, get me a coffee."

She ignored his request. "I'll be back in fifteen minutes. Make him rest."

Ryan snorted. "Yeah. I can make Daniel do stuff. You know what he does for a living, right?"

"Stop being an ass. Just look after him. I'll be back soon."

She listened for her brother to lock his door behind her then hurried down to the street. She walked to the shop as fast as she could without attracting attention. Lifting the payphone receiver, she paused. Who to call? If she called 911, they might not get the message to the right people quickly enough. But she didn't know who else to contact.

The Philadelphia police had been investigating Su-jin's murder, though Sarah didn't know which precinct. But the buried body was in a public park. Another agency would have jurisdiction, wouldn't they? Only she had no idea which one. State police? Park security?

In the end, she decided her only choice was 911. An innocent bystander would only know to call 911 anyway.

When the operator answered, Sarah said, "I need to report something anonymously. I'm not sure…I saw a guy in the woods at Ridley Creek State Park. He was digging and the smell…the smell was horrible like something dead. And he had a rifle."

"Probably just a hunter ma'am." The operator's voice was reasonable and calm.

"No, no really." Sarah gave her the exact location of the body and said, "I swear, I thought I saw a human hand sticking out of the ground." That little lie would probably come back to haunt her, but she didn't know how else to make sure they investigated.

"You're sure, ma'am?"

"It was dark. But I swear, it looked like a hand. And this guy was digging. I was so scared. He looked kind of familiar, but I can't say from where. Maybe I saw him on TV? I don't know. He just looked…familiar, something recent. I was too scared, I couldn't place him."

She didn't actually want to give Williams' name because a human witness wasn't likely to make the connection. But if the police were considering someone *known*, they'd have even more reason to look at him.

"Please," she said, making sure she sounded as panicked as she felt. "Please, send someone. The smell…It was a human hand, I swear." She made a gagging noise, hoping she could sell this story. If this didn't work, Williams would have time to move the body and no one would ever find out.

"How did you see this, ma'am?"

"I was…hiking." She remembered her and Daniel's cloths and improvised. "My boyfriend and I were…hiking. We heard something…I've never smelled anything like that. Please, you have to send someone."

"The location again, ma'am?"

Sarah gave her the exact directions again. "Please, please, please. I'm really worried."

"Okay, ma'am. Just try to stay calm. I'll contact the appropriate authorities. It's likely he was just burying an animal, but we'll send someone out to check."

Sarah hung up and stared at the phone. Damn, damn, damn. This wasn't going to work. Williams would get away.

And there was nothing she could do about it right now. If she didn't get to the Run, the elders would send Trackers to find her and bring her in. They'd question her. Everything would fall apart. Daniel might get into trouble.

Fuck! She had to run. She'd have to wait until afterwards to find out if the human authorities followed up on her call or not. If they didn't, then Sarah would find another way to draw their attention to Williams. She'd stalk him until he gave her the leverage she needed to have him arrested and convicted of murder.

She no longer wanted him dead, but she still wanted him to suffer. She wanted justice. And she'd make sure Su-jin got that justice in whatever form Sarah could arrange.

* * *

Ryan was heading out the door by the time she got back to his apartment. He snatched the coffee from her hand as he moved, saying, "Stay as long as you need. I'll be back later."

Sarah stilled him with her hand on his arm. "Thanks. What you did…it means a lot. Really."

"Do me a favor. Next time you visit, don't bring wounded tigers." He winked, then he was gone."

Turning to Daniel, she saw he'd shifted back to human while she was gone. He was also wearing a pair of Ryan's sweats and a t-shirt—clothes that were about two sizes too small. The material plastered to his muscles like a second skin, and for a few moments, Sarah could only stare.

She licked her lips and had to force down the urge to throw him onto the couch and rip those too-small clothes off of him.

"How did it go?" he asked without preamble, pulling her from her lustful thoughts.

"I'm not sure if the 911 operator believed me or not. I pretended to be a hiker—who'd been 'hiking' with her boyfriend." Her cheeks heated, though she wasn't sure why. "I wanted an excuse for our clothes being left in the woods."

He raised his brows. "Good thinking. Although if they find the blood from my wound, we might have a problem, even if the clothes weren't."

Ah hell. She'd forgotten all about the blood they'd left behind. They didn't need another complication that could get them all confined.

"Why do you think the 911 operator didn't believe you?" he asked.

"She brought up the very logical option that I might have been seeing things. She agreed to have it checked out, but I don't know if she was placating me."

"You tried. If we don't hear anything on the news about a found body, we'll try another way to get their attention."

If Williams didn't move the body in the meantime.

"Why did you shift already? It hasn't been an hour."

"Close enough. There are things to do. I can't convalesce all day."

A niggling of hurt clawed at her chest. "You were worried I wouldn't come back?"

"No." But he didn't meet her gaze.

So much for trust, she thought. She had ruined things. Without trust, what did they have? She swallowed hard.

"I'll put in a call too," he said.

"You think a second 911 call will help?"

"I've got a friend on the force here in Philly. I'll touch base with him. He'll make sure the story is taken seriously."

"Another human friend?"

He raised his brows. "I have a number of them, yes."

"But…"

"I have a lot of contacts, Sarah. They often come in handy while doing my job."

"But a human?"

"Sarah, I can't really discuss it now."

Hurt, she turned away from him. "We should get going. I need to go back to my place and get ready for the Run."

She led him to the truck. Unease and uncertainty settled between them and remained there all the way to her apartment.

As she turned to get out of the truck, Daniel stilled her with a hand on her arm. "I'll see you tomorrow night." He paused, then, "You'll be okay getting there on your own?"

Silly question. She always traveled there on her own. But she appreciated his concern. "I'll be fine."

Now that he was no longer bleeding and she was no longer on the hunt for bloody revenge, things were awkward between them. The easy companionship they'd built during the last seven cycles buckled under the strain of everything that had happened, all the things still unsaid.

"We'll talk more…soon," Daniel said.

"Sure."

There was so much more to say and discuss, but as she turned away, her heart broke. He didn't trust her. She'd lost him and had no idea how to get him back.

* * *

"Hey, Dan, what's happening?" Detective Peter Kelly said when he answered his phone.

Daniel made his call from a truck stop payphone as he headed out of Philly on his way to the location deep in the central Appalachians where the Run would take place. He planned to stop midway to get some sleep, so he could finish healing and be well rested to run for Sarah. He wasn't sure she'd let him catch her this time, but he intended to be strong enough to chase.

"I need you to check into something, Pete. An anonymous 911 call was placed this morning, early around seven a.m., with information about something buried just inside Ridley Creek State Park. I need you to make sure that's looked into."

"Want to tell me why?"

"Nope. But it's important."

"What kind of important? I can't just go poking my nose into a report of domestic disturbance or something. Especially when it's nowhere near my jurisdiction."

"Serious important. Murder."

The line was quiet for a long moment. "You're gonna have to give me more, Dan. Something…"

"Can't. Sorry. Wish I could. Just pay attention to this particular call. Don't write it off. Make sure the state police investigate."

"One of these days, you're gonna explain all this mysterious shit to me."

"Nope," Daniel said with a half grin. "Thanks, Pete."

"Yeah, yeah."

Pete hung up without further comment. Daniel put the phone handset back into its cradle and stared at it for a moment. He'd done what he could. Pete was a good cop. He wasn't working on Su-jin's case, but he was a smart detective. He'd know what to do, who to talk to.

That was all Daniel could do for now. If this didn't work…

He'd come up with another plan. Something that didn't endanger Sarah this time.

As he climbed back into his truck, the thought of what might have happened last night made him sick to his stomach. He'd acted on instinct that went beyond his logical thinking when he'd jumped in front of Sarah and taken that bullet. He'd known somewhere deep inside that she was in trouble and had acted without thought.

Now, though, with time to consider all the things that might have been…

He was sick from the possibilities. She could have been shot, or worse, killed. Williams could have found them while Daniel was incapacitated. They could have been intercepted trying to get back to the truck. Williams could have caught them on the highway and seen Sarah.

Daniel's hands clenched around the steering wheel and he had to force himself to breathe deeply to calm his rising panic. None of those things had happened, but the possibility that they could have made his heart pound.

At least Sarah had had enough sense to give Williams a false name. He hadn't seen them last night, so he had no reason to assume they were the ones in the woods. In fact, if he'd seen anything, it was only their animals, so there was even less reason for him to think of Daniel and Sarah in relation to that run through the trees.

They were safe. Sarah was safe. And they'd done what they could to turn the police's attention toward Williams and that poor buried body. There was nothing else he could do now.

Unless he skipped the Mate Run.

The idea of Sarah with another man cut a deeper hole than the bullet had. If Daniel didn't show, she'd *have* to choose a mate for this cycle. She couldn't just run around for three days and not let someone catch her. Well she could, but would she? And what if she got pregnant by another man?

The thought returned—what if she didn't want him there? Would she still let *him* catch her?

The ache in his chest far outweighed the ache in his shoulder. He had to accept her decision—if she didn't choose him this time, he had to let her go. But he didn't have to make it easy for her.

If the cops didn't do anything about their tip, Daniel would find another way to turn their attention on the crazy man. After the Run. He'd stalk Williams until the end of time if that's what it took. For Sarah. To give her some sort of satisfaction, some vague kind of revenge.

First, though, he would run. He'd fight for the woman he loved. If she no longer wanted him, he'd deal with it when the time came.

He wasn't sure how, but for her, he was prepared to do anything. Even give her up.

Chapter Twelve

Daniel stalked through the trees in tiger form, his senses open. He felt Sarah to the west and two other males were closing on her. He didn't immediately run to intercept them. Instead, he waited, scenting the air. Sarah's unique, flavorful smell carried to him, highlighted like a glowing beacon by the indefinable addition of her estrous. So delicious and tempting, so addictive.

But she'd let other males get close. She might have chosen someone else this time, and if he got too near, he'd challenge the other males. He wouldn't be able to help himself. So he waited, resisting her call for as long as he could.

He crouched low and growled when he felt another three males drawing close to her location. What was she doing, letting so many get that close? Would she take more than one this cycle? Females did sometimes. But Sarah hadn't before.

Though she'd never let anyone but him catch her before either, so he was in no position to guess what she might do now.

Unable to hold off any longer, he stalked closer to her location. And then he felt her move, fast. One instant, she was being surrounded by five different males, the next, she was racing in his direction.

Daniel roared and charged toward her, no longer in complete control of his reactions. She veered off to the south and he followed, racing over the uneven ground as he chased her. The other males also joined the chase, but they were further behind now, not near enough to catch her.

She was his.

He studied her run, judged her direction, then changed his, angling around to cut her off. She changed direction again, foiling his plan, and he thrilled at the challenge. Sarah was no easy prey.

He adjusted his plan again, speeding so fast through the trees a human observer would see little more than a white flash. Fortunately, this place was as isolated as they could get from humans, so deep into the Appalachian mountains very few human hunters or hikers ever made it this far. It was a location frequently used for Mate Runs because of that.

And after seven cycles, Daniel knew the terrain as well as Sarah did.

He caught her by surprise when he burst out of the trees to block her path. She'd run in human form, which thrilled him—

they could only get pregnant in human form. She skidded to a halt and laughed when she saw him. Then she bolted in a new direction, not giving in too easily.

Her reaction spurred him on. He'd been so afraid she'd reject him this Run. Her playful teasing and encouragement lightened his soul, and he raced after her with the enthusiasm of a cub.

He cut her off again, this time jumping in front of her so suddenly, she fell into him. The feel of her weight against his side and back was a satisfaction all its own. With a laugh, she pushed away and started to jump into a new direction, but he moved in a tight circle around her, giving her nowhere to go.

Grinning at him, she shook her head. "Shift, my beautiful man. I'm caught."

He still sensed the other males, hovering close enough to be a problem. But Sarah simply knelt on the ground and stared at him, a gleam of anticipation in her eyes.

Her black hair hung in a straight cloud around her bare shoulders. Her small breasts drew his attention as he moved a little ways away to begin his shift. So beautiful. The night was warm and humid, and sweat glistened on Sarah's skin in the bare light from a crescent moon. They were in a small break in the trees, not enough to be a clearing, but enough to cast faint light over her lithe form. He wanted her so much he ached.

The shift only increased that ache, a low level of discomfort adding to his excitement and desire. He changed as quickly as was safe and then rose to his full height. She stared up at him with heat in her eyes, her gaze traveling over his body.

He could never resist the way she looked at him.

She was on her feet by the time he reached her, but she didn't touch him immediately. Her gaze dropped to his erection and she licked her lips. He growled and flexed his fingers. He wanted to touch her more than he wanted to breathe. But he held back, letting her lead the way this first time.

She smiled as she gripped his cock, stroking him in long, slow pulls. Jaw clenched to keep still, he watched her small hand moving, the feel of her skin like hot velvet.

"Does that feel good?" she asked.

He could only grunt in response. But it was enough to make her laugh. The sound brushed over his naked skin. A sharp spike of pleasure raced up his spine.

"I know what will feel even better," she sang, and dropped to her knees.

When her mouth closed over the tip of his cock, he dug his fingers into her hair, unable to keep from touching her any longer. The scent of their mutual desire rose up around him in a cloud of delicious sweetness and musk, mingling with the smell of pine, oak, and the rich soil. He closed his eyes to savor the feel of her wet mouth, the scents of sex and Sarah, and the wilderness around them.

She licked the length of him, then took just his tip into her mouth again, tonguing him before sliding all the way down. He wasn't going to last long this way, but he couldn't muster the strength to make her stop. His muscles quivered as her fingers brushed delicately over his ass. The combination of hard suck and soft touch made him see spots.

"Sarah…" Her name came out rough and low, his desperation a physical thing between them.

Her laughter vibrated over his cock and he gasped, on the brink of coming despite his best efforts.

"Up," he ordered. "Now."

She complied with a smug grin, licking her lips as she stared up at him.

God, he loved this woman. He lifted her off her feet, and she wrapped her legs around his waist, bumping her wet heat against his cock. He sucked in a breath, then lifted and lowered her until his erection settled at her entrance. He held her gaze, savoring the moment before thrusting up at the same moment as he dropped her down.

Her head fell back and she moaned loudly. He could listen to that sound for the rest of his life and never grow tired of it.

The advantage of his strength and her small stature meant he didn't need to lean against anything to fuck her this way. He gripped her ass and kept her balanced as she clenched and released, rising and falling onto his cock, her eyes narrowed to slits, her mouth parted. He was so enchanted by the sight of her, he actually forgot how close he'd been to orgasm. Every pant, every flare of her nostrils, every flutter of her lashes tied his soul up further. He'd never thought to love someone like this. She was beautiful, smart, strong…perfect for him.

And she'd chosen him again.

Keeping her balanced with one arm, he moved his other hand around to thumb her clit. Her inner muscles clamped around him hard. Her legs around his waist squeezed him tighter.

"Daniel," she panted. "Oh, yes. Please."

She moved faster, her eyes closed now. He watched with unabashed pleasure as her chest and face flushed, her breathing increased, her moans got louder. Sweat dripped down her temples, and beads of perspiration streaked over her chest, drawing his attention to her breasts.

"So fucking perfect," he said, his heart pounding in his chest. "Come, Sarah. Come for me."

"Yes."

She moved faster, her hands clenching his shoulders, her fingernails a sharp, delectable pain. Her inner muscles were so tight, his own building need for release suddenly bit down hard and he felt himself losing control. He adjusted his hold, pressed his thumb against her clit a little more firmly, and Sarah cried out as her body jerked and tightened.

He held out as long as he could, but watching her come, savoring the sight and the scent rising up between them, did him in. He closed his eyes and pumped into her hard, letting all his pent up fear and hurt go with a release that broke through him like an avalanche.

Long moments passed before he breathed normally again and brought his body back under his control. When he opened his eyes, Sarah was staring at him. She smiled and kissed him, angling her mouth over his.

And all was right in his world.

* * *

Sarah unwrapped her legs from Daniel's waist and slid to the ground, enjoying the sharp shocks of sensation as her sensitive skin glided over his hot, firm flesh. The brush of his body hair against all her most delicate parts sent little sparks of pleasure shooting through her.

"I'm so glad you're here with me," she murmured.

"God, that's a relief." He blew out a breath and kissed her, hard.

"You were worried?"

"Of course. What did you think?"

"That I'd ruined things."

"*You'd* ruined things?"

"By going after—"

Daniel put a hand over her mouth, stopping her. "I know we still have a lot to talk about, when it comes to all that, but…I'd like to forget about him for a few more hours. I just want to be with you, like it was before all this. We'll talk. I promise. But…"

"Oh Daniel, I'd love that. So much." She pulled his head down to hers and kissed him soundly.

The run had released a lot of her pent up anxieties. She'd felt powerful and sexy and strong. The frustration and helplessness plaguing her fell away under the control she exerted in the Run. Here she was in charge. Here she could take what she wanted and the outcome was in her hands.

And at that moment, what she wanted more than anything in the world was Daniel.

She wrapped herself up in his heat, basked in the mingling of their scents that created a uniquely perfect perfume. Relief and release warmed her muscles and lightened her heart. She poured all her attention and focus into the need and lust, and love, Daniel inspired, pushing everything else away. For now, for this moment, she simply enjoyed the freedom of having him all to herself, without worrying about anything else.

The other males still lurked in the forest at a distance. They would hover in the Run territory for a few more hours before giving up and going home. Knowing they were still out there added an element of excited danger to sex with Daniel that was almost exhibitionism. The others were witness to the power and strength of her bond with Daniel. And she wanted him again, wanted to rejoice in the passion between them.

Rubbing her body up against his, she felt him growing hard again. "Oh, good," she purred into his mouth, reaching down to wrap her fingers around his thickness.

His chuckle was choked and gravel rough. "Insatiable," he accused.

"For you? Yes."

He cupped her breasts and rubbed his thumbs over her raised nipples, sending bolts of sensation through to her core. She was more than ready for him, the satisfaction of her last orgasm a fading memory as the need built again.

He lifted his mouth from hers and looked around. Then he picked her up and carried her to a nearby fallen log, putting her back on her feet only when he'd cleared an area on the ground with his foot so she could stand in warm soil instead of on broken branches and fallen needles.

The padding on the bottom of their feet was harder and rougher than a human's, so she was perfectly able to move across the ground without hurting herself or being uncomfortable. But his care for her comfort made her heart beat a little harder.

"Turn around," he ordered. "Brace your hands here."

She complied with a hum of anticipation. Looking over her shoulder, she watched him studying her, his gaze on her ass, his hand unconsciously stroking his own cock. She loved watching him like this so much she could come without ever touching him. He looked up and caught her staring. His blue eyes were dark and heated, his expression full of intensity, his focus entirely on her.

She swallowed as her muscles trembled in reaction to his obvious desire.

He slid a hand down her spine, a gentle pass that made her arch and moan. Then he cupped her ass cheek and kneaded her flesh, coming up so close she felt the bump of his erection against her hip. His other hand swept up to her heat, his fingers going unerringly to her most sensitive flesh. As he teased her clit with one hand, he slid the hand on her ass under her and nudged her legs wider. She was so eager to have him in her, she clenched her teeth to keep from rushing him. This time, he would lead the way and she would take what he gave her.

She dropped her head back, arching her spine and letting her hair fall over her shoulders to tickle her skin. Sweat, musk, and sex, and that unique mix of pheromones, surrounded them like a fog.

"You like me here," he murmured against her ear as he slid his fingers through her slick folds, dipping his middle finger inside before pulling out to play with her clit.

"Yes," she groaned.

When he started pulling away, she gripped his wrist to keep him where he was. He laughed, his hot breath brushing her neck. She shivered but didn't release her hold. So much for letting him lead, she thought.

A moment later, she stopped thinking all together. He shifted to stand directly behind her and pulled her hips back until she felt the press of his cock against her entrance. The warm night air was still and heavy around them, and a light sheen of sweat coated her skin. All of it heightened her focus on Daniel's touch. With one hand still wrapped around the front of her, his fingers buried in her curls, he nudged her legs wider and slid his full length into her tight heat.

The slow entrance let her savor every thick inch of him until she felt his hips bump solidly against her ass. Then he moved, stroking in and out, creating an erotic friction that sent her climbing to orgasm fast. She didn't care. She let him take her, let him push her until she came with a cry that echoed in the trees.

He didn't give her time to come down before he pumped faster, harder, the sound of skin slapping against skin joining with her cries. Her clit was so sensitive now his touch almost hurt, but even that felt perfect, overwhelming, and wonderful.

She looked over her shoulder again so she could watch him lose control. The sight of his face tightening, sweat clinging to his hair and body, was the most beautiful thing she'd ever seen.

He slammed into her hard enough to bring her up on her toes and then his body went stiff, his muscles tightened, and she felt him pulse inside her as he groaned her name. He continued pumping into her as his muscles relaxed and his breathing slowed, then he pulled her up and wrapped his arms around her, his chest warm against her back.

She held his arms in place and relaxed into the strength and rightness of being with him.

"I'm glad we have three full days," she murmured as she dropped her head back against his shoulder.

"I'd prefer if we had a lifetime," he said against her temple.

"Me too."

She turned in his arms and kissed him, relieved beyond words. She'd lost sight of the future over the last week and a half. She hadn't been able to think of happiness or love or hope. Here in the deep forest, holding him close, their naked skin pressed tight together, their mingled scent a halo around them, she could consider the future again, and could believe in happiness and hope.

Daniel gave her something to look forward to, something to live for. And she loved him so much for that, she didn't have the words.

When her knees wobbled and she almost fell, she dropped back against the log and laughed. "Do you want to go to the cabin yet?" she asked.

There was a lovely little cabin maintained and kept tidy for the couples who ended up together after the Run. The cupboards were stocked and the bed always had fresh linen. But the freedom of the open air often kept couples outside, away from the cabin for at least the first day. She and Daniel were no exception.

"Not yet," he said. "But I do want you to sleep."

She raised her brows. "You're sure you want to sleep?"

"No. But you need to."

"I can keep up with you."

He snorted. "Oh, I'm well aware of that. I also know you haven't slept much lately and even you need a few hours."

He looked around then took her hand and led her into the trees.

"Have you slept?"

"A little. Last night."

"Ha. So you're the one who needs to sleep."

He grinned over his shoulder. "Maybe. Or maybe I just like the way you wake me up."

"Mmm." She liked waking him up, too.

He hunted around until he found a patch of soft mossy ground. After removing rocks and twigs, they snuggled down together. He held her close, face to face, his expression relaxed and happy.

She cupped his cheek and rubbed her thumb over his skin, smiling at the rough texture of scruff. When she closed her eyes, he kissed her forehead and settled her head under his chin. Wrapped up in his scent and heat, she found peace and slept deeply.

Chapter Thirteen

They spent the next two days in a blur of sex and fun, relaxation and renewal. They ate, they ran, they played, they splashed around in the nearby stream, they made love every chance they could. Just like the previous cycles, they abandoned the outside world completely and enjoyed each other.

The time healed something Daniel had thought broken, and his relief was overwhelming. When he stopped to consider what might have happened, it made his chest tight.

They very purposefully *didn't* discuss the future, the past, or anything to do with what had almost pulled them apart.

But as they took to the forest for their last night together, the future—their future—hovered in the back of Daniel's mind. Eventually, they'd need to talk about what had happened before the Run. They would have to decide what to do if their efforts to call attention to Williams had failed.

When they were a few hundred yards away from the cabin, Sarah looked over her shoulder at him, her smile slow and sultry. Daniel decided all those eventuallys could wait a little while longer. Without warning, she took off at a run, laughing as she disappeared into the trees.

He growled loud enough for her to hear, then charged after her. Her squeal of delight fired his blood.

They raced through the forest until Daniel decided enough was enough, then he cut her off and swept her into his arms. She screeched in surprise. She was a good hunter, but his job was to track and capture other tigers. He loved that he could surprise her even when she thought she had him beat.

She relaxed into his kiss without protest, and he savored the taste of her, trying to forget this was their last night together until her next cycle. He didn't want to give this up again, not after everything that had happened in the week before. He wanted to return to Philly with Sarah and never leave her side.

Impractical even if they could. He had a job to do. So did she. But oh how he wanted to spend the rest of his life with her in his arms.

He'd purposefully caught her in a small grass-covered clearing so when he brought her to the ground, the earth beneath them was as comfortable as the cabin bed. He held himself above her, most of his weight on his arms as he looked into her beautiful dark eyes.

He loved her so much his heart wanted to burst with the feeling. She cupped his face in her soft palms, and he opened his mouth to tell her, the emotion so close to the surface, he couldn't keep it in any longer. She stopped him with a kiss so delicious, he couldn't bring himself to break away from her even to say the words he needed to say.

As he settled between her thighs and slid into her heat, he swallowed her moans. His ability to think shattered the instant her hips flexed up to meet his. So he didn't try. He rocked into her, held her close and kissed her with everything he had.

And when she came apart in his arms, he knew she was his. They might not be able to make it formal yet, but she was his, fully and completely.

Nothing would come between them ever again.

* * *

They fell asleep outside, taking advantage of the freedom of their last night to simply be themselves in the beauty of this wild place. To his surprise, Daniel woke before Sarah. Since he rarely got to watch her sleep, he took advantage of the moment. She was beautiful. And his.

The warm night, and their naturally high body temperatures, made it pleasant and sensual lying naked outdoors with the woman he loved next to him.

Love.

He had to tell her. He should have told her before they fell asleep, but making love to Sarah robbed him of his ability to think clearly. He didn't want this cycle to end without her knowing, though. So much had happened, and come morning, they'd have to return to civilization and face reality again. He didn't want her going back to Philly without knowing exactly how he felt. That he loved her. That he *trusted* her.

She'd made it clear she had no intention of trying to kill Williams anymore. She'd be safe from the repercussions of that choice. So it was time for them to talk about their future.

In all the cycles of being together, trying to get pregnant so they could be a couple freely outside the Run, he'd never talked about what he wanted for them after…if they got pregnant. He hadn't wanted to bring the topic up during this cycle either, not while they were healing. But he couldn't separate from her this time without letting her know his intentions.

He brushed a strand of black hair away from her temple. When she woke, he'd tell her everything. The words burned in his chest, demanding to be released.

If she didn't love him yet…

He could live with that because she still wanted him. She'd still *chosen* him for this cycle. He had time to earn her love.

The sound of a branch breaking launched Daniel into a crouch, positioning himself between Sarah and the sound. He'd been so focused on Sarah, he had ignored any sign that someone was approaching. The area had been all theirs for the last few days, no humans or tigers anywhere nearby, so he'd stopped paying attention to his surroundings. A mistake he'd berate himself for later. He opened his senses and turned to face the intruder.

When Victor dropped from a tree at the edge of the clearing, grinning like a Cheshire cat, Daniel cursed aloud.

He sat back on the grass next to an alert Sarah and scowled at the smiling man. As his initial adrenaline rush eased, Daniel sensed Alexis approaching. She stepped out of the trees a moment later.

"What the hell are you doing here?" he demanded.

Victor raised his brows, and Alexis shook her head. "Sorry about that. He's developed this weird quirk. He loves sneaking up on Trackers, just to see if he can." She gave her husband a look, and he returned it completely unrepentant.

"Does he do that to you?" Daniel demanded.

She snorted. "He tries."

Victor signed something to her, his gaze narrowed, his smile confident. Alexis signed back with a casual shrug. To Daniel, she said, "He hasn't managed to sneak up on me yet. He keeps trying, though."

Daniel rubbed a hand through his hair and looked back at Sarah. "This is embarrassing. I shouldn't have let him do that." He shouldn't have let his guard down, even after days of being alone with her. Damn.

"You were distracted," Alexis allowed. "And he has gotten pretty good at being a sneaky bastard. I use him to help me train the younger cubs now, but he wasn't nearly this good when you were my student."

Victor scowled and signed something with a hard jerk of his hands. Alexis just smirked.

Sarah tried hiding a smile. Daniel groaned.

"What are you two doing here?" he asked again. He'd had entertaining ideas for waking Sarah in the same way she usually woke him during their time together. A surprise visit by his former mentor and her husband did *not* figure into his plan.

"We have some news we thought you'd be interested in before you head back tomorrow."

"It couldn't wait?"

"To be honest, I was afraid if we didn't tell you, one or both of you might launch into something stupid as soon as you left here."

"Williams" Daniel said, sitting a little straighter. Sarah edged forward, and he pulled her into his arms. He'd dreaded having to return to this topic, but Alexis was right. Tomorrow they'd have to face the reality of Williams again. Better to know what they were returning to.

"They found the body in the park behind his property. They've identified her."

"Wait," Sarah interrupted. "Where's Joseph? Has he… changed his mind about revenge, too?"

"Too?" Alexis asked, exchanging a look with Daniel.

"Long story," he told her. "But she's not trying to kill him anymore. Who was buried there?"

"Turns out," Alexis said, settling onto a tree stump just inside the clearing, "she was a chemist who worked for one of Williams' father's pharmaceutical companies."

"A chemist? As in…"

"Yeah, likely the woman who developed the drug for Williams. That's bugged me since we found out because there's no evidence of chemistry knowledge in his background. Makes more sense now."

"What makes you think she helped him develop the drug?" Sarah asked.

"At the moment, mostly instinct," Alexis allowed. "She's been missing for about a month, though the corner put her death at roughly two weeks ago."

"Son-of-a-bitch," Daniel muttered. Su-jin had been taken and murdered right around the same time as this other woman had died. But if the coroner was right, that meant this chemist had been held, and probably tortured, for two weeks. The idea made Daniel's stomach churn.

"Her colleagues told the police she'd been working on something secret," Alexis continued. "Claimed she was doing the work for 'an important company person', but wouldn't admit more. Seems she kept records though. Until her body was found, the authorities hadn't been able to get a warrant to look into those files. The company's lawyers wouldn't allow it. Now the police are going after the warrant."

"Will they get it?" Daniel asked.

"How did you learn all this?" Sarah asked at the same time.

Alexis answered Sarah first. "Daniel's not the only one with contacts in human law enforcement," she said with a slight lift of her shoulders. "I called in a favor." To Daniel, she said, "Not sure if they'll get the warrant. Depends entirely on the judge."

"Have they performed an autopsy yet?" Daniel asked.

"Finished the physical autopsy yesterday, and all the various lab tests are underway."

"They'll find the drug used on Su-jin in this woman," Daniel said with certainty.

"You recognized it?"

He nodded. "If she has records, if she names Williams in her notes, will that be enough to arrest him?"

Alexis pursed her lips. "Hopefully. It'll be enough to question him. They're definitely suspicious of him. They actually have been this whole time, according to my source, but even more so since Su-jin's body was stolen. Considering who his father is and the resources at his disposal, it seems the authorities think Williams is the most likely suspect to have arranged the theft of the body and all the evidence—something they assume only a person involved in her murder would do. None of the other suspects in Su-jin's murder could have arranged it. But they had nothing to go after Williams with that would make it past his lawyers. With luck, they'll find something now."

"So," Sarah said, "they'll go after him. He won't get away with this."

"Again, hopefully. They'll need indisputable evidence to get through those shark lawyers of his. But this is pretty suspect stuff. He'll be their focus now."

"Did Joseph take the news well?"

Victor and Alexis exchanged a look. Then Alexis shook her head and faced them again. "Joseph has been confined for his own good." The regret and resignation in her voice were almost physical things.

"Confined?"

Sarah sounded so surprised Daniel tightened his hold, trying to give her comfort.

"We couldn't talk him down. No matter what we did. When we got news of the chemist's body being discovered, I thought that would do it. But as we drove back to the elder's compound, Joseph broke away at a rest stop near Philly. He actually tried reaching the city on foot. Took Victor almost an hour to catch him and bring him back. And it was full daylight!" She sighed. "He just wouldn't listen."

Victor signed something to her and she signed back.

"We tried," she said aloud. "He was spewing a lot of hate when they took him away. Not sure he'll ever forgive us."

Victor turned away, facing into the trees so Daniel could only see the side of his face. But the tightness of his jaw and the flex of his fists said a lot about how the man felt.

"They've put him in the same place as Elizaveta's son, Ivan. It's comfortable enough, not as harsh as some of the cells."

Victor signed again and Alexis said, "Like the place Victor lived with his mother when she was confined. It's for Joseph's own good. But it sucks. A lot."

"Maybe he'll calm down once Williams is arrested."

Alexis dipped her head to one side in a slight shrug. "Maybe. He still wants to kill the man with his bare hands and nothing short of that seems to be enough for him. We'll see what happens."

"Thanks for coming up to give us a status report," Daniel said.

"Whatever you both did," Alexis said as she rose, "it managed to focus the investigation on Williams without giving yourselves away."

Victor signed something a little more urgent and Alexis nodded. "Oh, yeah, well…" To them, she said, "There was the blood found near a couple sets of clothes."

"Shit," Daniel said. "I knew that would come back and bite us in the ass."

"My source said they assumed the clothes were from the couple who caught Williams 'burying something'. The blood…"

"Will have to disappear, won't it?" Daniel was already contemplating how quickly he could get back to Philly and do what he'd done before—steal evidence.

"Turns out," Alexis said, breaking into his thoughts, "they immediately checked to see if it was human or animal since there's hunting allowed in Ridley Creek. They didn't want to waste time analyzing samples that had nothing to do with the body. Labs are too busy. And when they discovered the blood was animal blood they set it aside."

"Did they find out what kind of animal?" Daniel asked.

"Doesn't work that way," Sarah put in. "Their initial tests would just be whether or not the blood was human."

"And since it wasn't, they had no reason to analyze further," Alexis said. "Thankfully. So we should be safe. After a couple of weeks, when they're not as focused on this case, I'll make sure those samples disappear and that the elders don't find out about them. In the meantime, we're okay." Her gaze jumped between them. "Which one of you was injured?"

"Me," Daniel admitted. "Shot."

"Through and through?" Alexis asked.

"Sarah's brother cut the bullet out."

Alexis' gaze narrowed. "He good with secrets?" she asked Sarah. "Because if he's not, it's your ass. The elders will be really pissed if they find out you were together outside the Run and messing around with Williams."

"Ryan will take the secret to his grave," Sarah said confidently.

Daniel was inclined to agree, even though his acquaintance with Sarah's brother had been brief. The man's scent held a difficult to describe element that announced "trustworthy" to Daniel's tiger and his Tracker instincts. He'd never been able to fully explain the way he scented such things—not all tigers could even do it—but it had helped him in his years of work as a Tracker, and he knew he was right in his assessment now. Ryan loved his sister. He wouldn't do anything to hurt her. He'd keep their secret to protect her. Daniel liked that about the younger man.

"You okay now?" Alexis asked him.

"Fine. All healed up."

"Good. So then, nothing to lead the authorities to our people, no reason for anyone else to get in trouble." She put a hand on Victor's shoulder. "Come on. Let's leave the love birds in peace so they can enjoy their last night here."

As they started back into the trees, though, Alexis paused and glanced back. "Congratulations, by the way."

Daniel frowned.

"You haven't noticed yet?" Alexis laughed. "Looks like you'll be loosing a lot of sleep in about eight months. I better be invited to the wedding." She waved and disappeared into the trees, Victor a silent shadow beside her.

Daniel stared after them for a long moment as what Alexis said sank in. Then he pulled in a deep breath and realized…

He faced Sarah. She was wide-eyed, her hands on her stomach, her nostrils flaring as she breathed in the new, flowery, soft scent that mixed so seamlessly with their combined essences neither of them had noticed.

Now that he was paying attention, Daniel was astonished he'd missed it.

"You're pregnant," he whispered and reached out to place his hand over hers.

She met his gaze, her dark eyes still wide. And then she smiled. A slow, shy, wondrous smile that filled Daniel's heart to bursting.

"I love you," he said, unable to keep the words in any longer. "I should have told you before, cycles ago. I was afraid you'd think it was too soon and choose someone else. But I do love you."

She let loose a huge sigh. "That's a relief."

"A relief?" He raised his brows. Not exactly the reaction he'd expected.

"Like I said, our first night here, I was afraid I'd ruined everything with my need for revenge. You didn't trust me, and how can you love someone you don't trust? Then you came to the Run, and I hoped any feelings you might have developed for me before—beyond lust—could be fixed now. I thought we were on our way to fixing them. But I didn't think you loved me."

He cupped her face in his palms and made sure she was looking him in the eyes when he said, "I love you and nothing, *nothing*, will change that. Do you understand? I couldn't stop loving you even if I wanted to. But I don't want to. I love you desperately. Why the hell else would I have risked losing you to keep you from hurting yourself?"

"Daniel." She launched into his arms, with so much strength and passion, she knocked him backward.

He hit the ground with a grunt, then laughed as she sprawled across him and covered his face with kisses. When she got close to his mouth, he captured her roving lips in a proper, deep kiss, filled with all the emotion he'd held in check for much too long.

She settled across him, her legs straddling his waist, her heat warm and wet against his lower abdomen. His reaction was immediate and intense.

He'd wanted her from the first moment he'd seen her and now she was his—freely and completely outside the Run. He could love her every day. Something he intended to do for the rest of his life, if she'd let him.

She wiggled back a little and her ass bumped up against the tip of his erection. "Oh, good," she said, with a distinct purr in her voice.

She rose up and gripped his cock in her small, strong hand, positioning him at her entrance before sliding onto him, wrapping him in her heat and wetness. He gripped her hips and closed his eyes, memorizing the feel of her as she rode him, the smell of their scents mixing and blending. That added earthy element with just a hint of fresh flowers, the note that allowed them to be together now.

He opened his eyes and caught her gaze as she watched him, a small smile tilting her lips up.

Beautiful.

His.

He slid his hands up her waist to cup her breasts. She dropped her head back, letting her hair slip over her shoulders and fall down her back. In the bare light filling the clearing, she was a stunning mix of light and shadow. He'd never wanted a woman more.

She rocked against him faster, her inner muscles clenching his cock until he felt his control slipping. This was a celebration and he wanted her to come with him. He slid one hand down the center of her stomach to the place where their bodies joined and pressed his thumb against her clit. She groaned, gripping his wrist to hold him in place. Even as he felt his own orgasm rising up, her muscles clenched, her breathing sped, and when he couldn't hold back any longer, he let go just as he felt her come. Their mutual cries echoed through the trees.

As her orgasm eased, she collapsed forward, a warm weight pressed against his chest. He wrapped his arms around her and squeezed as tightly as he dared.

"You're okay, right?" he asked, suddenly worried about the baby. Their baby.

She sat up a little and frowned down at him. "If you can't tell I'm *okay* by now, you haven't been paying attention for the last seven…eight cycles now."

"No. I mean the baby. We didn't…hurt you or anything?"

She laughed and snuggled down against him, pushing her head up under his chin. "Of course not, silly man. We can have sex right up to the point where I go into labor and we won't hurt the baby. So long as the pregnancy is healthy."

"Then we'd better make sure you stay healthy."

"Absolutely."

She was quiet for a moment and he could practically hear her thinking.

Then, "We've never really discussed…what would happen when I got pregnant."

"Well, we'll get married of course."

She sat up again. "Of course?"

"Yes, of course. I love you. I want to marry you and have as many babies with you as we can make."

She smiled softly and leaned in to kiss him.

"Daniel." She spoke between kisses. "Yes, by the way."

"Yes?"

"Yes, I'll marry you."

Daniel felt the world fall away until only they existed. A perfect moment he would value for the rest of his life.

Chapter Fourteen

They returned to Sarah's apartment in Philadelphia the next afternoon. Since he traveled for his job, and she worked in Philly, they decided to live there. Eventually, he'd have to collect his things from the small house he kept in West Virginia near the elders' compound, and they needed to find something bigger than her one bedroom apartment so they'd have space for the baby.

"Babies," she'd reminded him with a grin. Because she intended to have as many with Daniel as she could.

She was so content, so satisfied with the direction her life was headed even memories of Su-jin left her more melancholy and sad than angry now. The anger was still there. She still hated Williams with every fiber of her being because he'd robbed her of her best friend.

But she could also imagine Su-jin's reaction to the news of Sarah's pregnancy. She could practically hear her friend's squeal of delight, feel her tight hug. So she kept that image in the front of her mind, to comfort herself, and because it was what Su-jin would want her to do.

Somehow, the pleasant thoughts seemed to honor her friend in a way revenge couldn't.

She half-listened in when Daniel called the elders' secretary to pass on the message that she was pregnant, and she and Daniel were getting married. Her heart beat a little faster as she heard him say all that aloud. It was real! They were going to be married and have a family.

She was still getting used to the idea and giddy with the reality of it.

When Daniel asked about Joseph, her excitement dimmed a little. If she went to talk with him, would he calm a little? They probably wouldn't let her near Joseph yet, but as soon as he was thinking rationally…

She had gone to Joseph once before knowing he'd want revenge too, knowing he'd go with her to kill Williams. Even though Joseph would have hunted the man by himself if she hadn't approached him, Sarah still felt a guilty pang of responsibility for putting him in this situation.

As she put together a hearty late lunch of soup and sandwiches for herself and Daniel, she heard him call Alexis and then his cop friend to check on the progress of the case. She couldn't hear nearly enough detail in that last conversation, though, so when he joined her in her small kitchen, she immediately grilled him for information.

"Well, what's happening? Have they brought Williams in for questioning? Did they get the warrant for the chemist's computer files? Have they linked the drug to him?"

Daniel raised a hand to still her onslaught. "They're still investigating." He settled into a chair at her small, two person table. "But you'll be happy to know they did get the warrant early this morning for the computer files. According to Pete, the files implicate Williams directly with the development of the drug. He's officially a person of interest."

"That's good, right?" She set a huge sandwich piled with various deli meats in front of him.

"It's a start. They still have a lot of the files to go through since they just got them. It's enough to bring Williams in for questioning, though. Pete said they're working on that now."

"Working on that? Meaning…"

"They don't know where he is exactly, so they're looking for him, talking with his lawyers. He's probably just hiding at one of his daddy's houses somewhere, waiting for the lawyers to rescue his sorry ass."

She poured their soup into two bowls and set those on the table. "Will the lawyers be able to?"

Daniel shrugged as he picked up his sandwich. "Hard to say. Depends on what the chemist's records reveal in the end, and what the tests from her autopsy show."

"What if he's left the country?" Williams had more than enough resources to disappear to a non-extradition country. She sat across from Daniel and spooned up soup as she considered that little complication.

"That'll make things harder," Daniel conceded. "We'll just have to wait and see."

"I hate waiting."

"You're a scientist. Don't you have to wait on results of tests all the time?"

"Entirely different," she said with a lift of her chin.

He smiled and she lost her train of thought. He was hers. *Hers*. Freely now. How long would it be before that settled in, she wondered.

"I've asked Pete to stop by, if you don't mind," Daniel said. "I didn't want to talk too much on the phone where we could be heard, but I want to learn more about the tests they're running on the chemist's blood and what they've found so far in her files. I want to make *sure* they find the drug Williams used."

"He'll tell you about evidence in an active investigation?" Daniel spoke highly of his contact, Pete, when he'd told her about the man while they were driving back to Philly. A man that dedicated to his job didn't sound like the kind of person who would break rules, even for a friend.

"He knows I'll keep it to myself," Daniel said. "And he kind of owes me a favor."

"What for?"

Daniel frowned a little. "I kept him from getting run over by the car of a fleeing murder suspect. Long story. Anyway, he won't tell me anything that might compromise the case. But we can discuss hypothetical tests that could be run to check for anything they might find in her files without hurting anything."

"Daniel, does he know…does he know you're different?"

"He thinks I'm a bounty hunter. All my human contacts in the various law enforcement agencies think the same thing. It's a good cover and explains a lot." He shrugged. "Essentially, it's not far from the truth."

As they ate, she considered his job. She'd never worried about him before, never stopped to consider how his work might affect their lives. Now that they were having a baby, she realized his job put him in a lot of danger.

"I really hate to bring this up," she said, not even sure how to broach the subject.

"What's wrong?"

"It's just…I fell in love with you knowing exactly what you do and who you are. But with the baby coming, I'm worried about you getting killed, and I don't know what to do about that." She held up a hand when he opened his mouth. "I'm not asking you to change jobs or anything like that. And I know you're good at what you do, so I trust you not to get yourself killed, but…stuff happens." She squeezed her face up in an embarrassed scowl. "I don't know what I'm saying. Ignore me. I must be getting hit with hormones already."

He reached across the table and took her hand, squeezing lightly. "It's perfectly valid for you to worry. Even more so after what happened to Su-jin. I do have a dangerous job and things do happen. You're marrying a man who hunts other tigers for a living. I won't dismiss your worry, but I am good at what I do. I've been trained by the best. I'm not easy to kill."

"I know." She nodded fast and pulled in a shaky breath. "I know. I'll adapt. I promise."

He kissed her knuckles just as the doorbell rang, interrupting what she wanted to say next. Just as well, because she wasn't sure what she wanted to say next.

"I'll get it," she said. "Finish your meal. What does Pete look like?"

"Tallish, mid-forties, dark blond hair. Reminds me of a young Colombo."

"Who?"

"TV detective?"

She shook her head. "Never heard of him."

"Oh, you have missed out on some excellent classic television, my love. But don't worry. I'll introduce you."

"If you say so." She chuckled as she went to the front door and looked out the peephole. A dark blond haired man stood with his back to her door. She sucked in a deep breath to pull in his scent as she opened the lock and realized a second too late the smell of the man outside was much too familiar.

For an instant, shock kept her from reacting. Williams spun and kicked in the door. She leapt away, avoiding the swinging door easier than any human would have, but her momentary shock had let a crazy man gain access to her home.

She didn't know how he'd found her, but her hackles rose, and a low growl rumbled in her throat. Rather than the fear she knew he expected, her anger surged back. This man had killed her best friend and shot her future husband. He'd made a serious mistake coming here.

He didn't seem to recognize his mistake, though because he smirked at her. "You think you could fool me with a fake last name?" he said, smug and confident. "I recognized you from the bar, you little bitch. I know you're that other bitch's friend."

Daniel launched out of the kitchen and landed in front of Sarah before she could attack. Whether he was protecting her or keeping her from ripping out Williams' throat, she wasn't sure.

She couldn't shift now that she was pregnant—she'd lose the baby if she did—but she was still stronger and faster than a mere human man, and his gloating, arrogant, insane face made her see red. Instinct to keep her baby far away from him was the only thing keeping her from pushing Daniel aside.

"Figures you'd be here," Williams said to Daniel.

He hadn't seemed to notice that Daniel moved faster than he should have been able to, or if he did, he didn't find it surprising.

That couldn't be good.

"You two are responsible for all this, aren't you?"

"For what?" Daniel asked, his voice deep and quiet.

"The cops. That body. That was you in the woods. Who did I shoot?" He narrowed his gaze. "You." He nodded at Daniel. "You keep jumping in front of her." He ran his gaze over Daniel's body. "Damn. Guess I didn't hit anything vital. Too bad."

"Since I'm not sporting any bullet holes," Daniel said, "you'd have a pretty hard time implicating me, or Sarah, in anything. Not to mention trying to explain why you think we might have been there in the first place. Or why you shot me."

Williams narrowed his eyes and stalked closer. "I know you know. But you can't stop me. My father will take care of this little…hiccup. Then you're both dead."

"What, too scared to try killing us without drugging us first?" Sarah shot, too angry and disgusted to hold her tongue. She sucked in another breath to say more and caught a faint whiff of that strange medicinal smell from the chemist's body. For the first time since Williams barged in, she hesitated. He actually had brought that drug into her home. Shit.

"Know about that, huh?" he asked. "How?" He sounded genuinely curious, as if it was a particularly interesting puzzle but nothing dangerous to him. "Seems I've made a few mistakes. But don't worry. I'm learning. I'm getting much, much better."

Sarah's stomach rolled as what he said sank in. "Have there been more?"

He grinned without actually admitting anything. It made her want to throw up.

"What are you doing here?" Daniel demanded.

Williams' gaze jumped to Sarah. "Well, I had hoped to find you alone. We never did finish our date."

Sarah lunged forward. The drug wasn't in his hands. She could kill him before he got anywhere near it. But Daniel stopped her, blocking her with his entire body.

"Such fire," Williams said. "Your little friend was fierce like that. She took a lot. A lot. And I can't help but think you'd be just as exciting. Something about you…"

Sarah's tiger roared. The sound that ripped from her throat was both anguish and rage and not quite human.

Williams just laughed. "Yes, something very interesting there. A mystery. I love mysteries. I can't wait to spend more time with you." His gaze jumped to Daniel. "You'll never be safe, you know. I'll be back for her. And you won't be able to stop me."

"Wouldn't count on that." Daniel's voice had gone almost inhuman sounding now, too.

Sarah glanced at him and realized he was only barely in control of his own rage. But if he killed the human…She gripped his arms and very quietly said, "Don't, Daniel."

His big body trembled, his muscles tensed, but he didn't move any closer to Williams.

"You two think you're so smart." Williams snarled and stalked closer. "You can't stop me. And I have plenty of time for you."

Sarah couldn't believe he was crazy enough to attack without a weapon. Right up until the instant he lunged at Daniel, fists swinging. Daniel must have been surprised by the ridiculous move, too, because he just stood there and took a punch to the face. The blow knocked his head to one side and might have thrown a human man sideways.

Daniel was no human.

He looked back at Williams, and before the man could throw another punch, Daniel backhanded him, sending him flying across the room to slam into a wall. Williams hit so hard, the drywall behind him cracked. He slid to the floor like a rag doll, eyes closed, then didn't move.

"Shit," Sarah said, starting forward. "Oh Daniel, you didn't kill him, did you?"

"No, Sarah, wait!"

But panic for what would happen to Daniel sent her rushing to Williams' side to check his pulse. As she leaned over him, he opened his eyes and grabbed her arm, a sick smile spreading over his face.

He jerked her in front of him and looked around her at Daniel, who was moving toward them. "Ah-ah," Williams said. "Back off or I break her neck."

Sarah stared at Daniel. His anger was a living thing in the room, his frustration evident in the flexing muscles of his jaw. She was more irritated than scared. But knowing Williams had that drug somewhere on him kept her from acting rashly again. She kept her gaze on Daniel and her senses on Williams, waiting for an opening.

Williams used the wall at his back to rise while still keeping her in front of him like a shield. Stupid, stupid man, she thought. She almost laughed when she realized he probably thought she was the stupid one. Little did he know. Without that drug, he was the one in trouble. She didn't care how crazy he was or what heightened skills his psychosis gave him, he'd messed with the wrong tigress.

"Catch a tiger by the toe," she murmured.

"What?" he snapped, his breath hot and wet against her cheek.

"I'm about to holler, and you'd better let me go," she said.

He laughed. "Now now, little one. We're going to walk out of here, and you're going to accompany me to the airport. Call the cops," he said to Daniel, "and you won't even recognize her body when I dump it."

Williams edged toward the door. He held her with one hand on her arm and stroked his fingers down her cheek with his other hand.

Daniel tracked them as they moved, but he didn't get closer. She held his gaze, letting him see she wasn't scared. Williams hadn't pulled out any syringes yet. She might not be able to turn tiger, but she still was one, and her anger was matched only by the fierce protectiveness she felt for her growing baby. This man would not threaten their lives. If she had to break every bone in his body—without killing him—she would.

"You," Williams said against her temple as he backed toward the gaping door, "are going to be a good little girl all the way to my car. You're going to walk out of here nice and quiet. If you struggle, if you resist, by the time I'm done with him, your hero there will beg me to kill him."

Actually, Sarah thought, breaking every bone in Williams' body sounded like a wonderful option.

She reached across her body and grabbed the fingers holding her arm. Then she squeezed, with all her strength. Williams cried out as she heard his bones crunch.

He punched her in the side of the head, hard enough, she dropped her grip on his fingers. Daniel shouted her name. Williams moved to punch her again, but she ducked under the blow, spun to face him, grabbed his uninjured fist and squeezed again until more bones cracked. He screamed and lunged forward, forcing her to stumble back or fall on her ass.

She regained her footing just as he swung his free arm toward her. Daniel stopped that blow and wrenched Williams' arm around. More bones shattered.

And then a new, calm voice from the doorway froze them all in place. "Well, well. What do we have here?"

Chapter Fifteen

Sarah dropped the hand she was still crushing and stepped back from Williams, facing the new potential threat, ready to attack. The person in the door was tallish, with dark blond hair and a generally rumpled appearance, despite the fact that he wore a suit. Detective Peter Kelly, she thought, and relaxed her stance.

He had a hand on the butt of his gun, but hadn't pulled it from his shoulder holster. Yet.

"Mr. Williams," he said. "Interesting finding you here of all places."

"These two attacked me," Williams screeched. "I'm pressing charges. They were going to kill me!"

"Now," Pete said, without taking his hand from his gun, "seems to me, you're in Dr. Chu's apartment. And I did just hear you threaten to kill Mr. Borowski if Dr. Chu didn't cooperate with you taking her *from* her apartment. That speaks strongly in favor of them defending themselves. Doesn't it, Dan?"

"Oh, definitely," Daniel said. "Self-defense all the way." In Williams' ear, Daniel said, "You're not the only one with connections." To Pete, he said more loudly, "Think we might have broken some bones here, Pete. Better call an ambulance."

"On it. Should get here right alongside my backup." He pulled a cell phone from his pants' pocket, flipped it open and hit a button all without taking his eyes off the situation. He did, however, take his hand off his gun.

"I don't know what you think you heard," Williams said to Pete, noticeably trembling, sweat dripping down his cheeks. "But you've got it wrong. They broke my arm, my hands! For no reason! You have to arrest them."

"Not how it works, Mr. Williams," Pete said. He flipped his phone closed. "But I do have some questions for the lot of you. Perhaps we better put you on opposite sides of the room until the ambulance arrives."

"You can't just let them go! My father will have your badge."

"He broke in," Sarah said, speaking up for the first time. "Kicked in my door. And you heard him threaten us. He was trying to kidnap me. We were in fear for our lives." Only a little fib, she thought. Fear wasn't exactly the word she'd use to describe her feelings as she'd broken Williams' bones. But Pete didn't need to know the complete truth.

"Hmm," Pete said. "Sounds like this wasn't a friendly visit, Mr. Williams."

"You might want to check his pockets, too, Pete," Daniel put in. "Carefully, though. Might be a sharp weapon."

Pete raised his brows. "Seeing as how this is a breaking and entering situation, with a potential kidnapping, I will ask you to stand still for a pat down, Mr. Williams."

Williams' eyes narrowed, but then he put his arms out to the side, despite the pain he had to be in.

Pete very carefully patted Williams down, finding a capped syringe in one of his pants pockets.

"Huh. What have we here, Mr. Williams? You often bring syringes to the homes of young ladies you *aren't* threatening? Cause I know you aren't diabetic."

"Think you might find that's got a familiar drug in it, Pete," Daniel said, without taking his eyes off Williams.

"Suspect we'd better have this tested then."

The sound of sirens approaching and cars pulling up to the street below drew Sarah's attention. But neither Daniel nor Pete took their focus off Williams.

A few minutes later, a couple of uniformed police officers knocked at the doorframe. Pete called them in. "I need a bag for this." He held up the syringe. "Careful with that now," he said as the officer sealed the evidence bag with the syringe inside.

"That was planted," Williams said with a smirk. "My lawyers will have that tossed out before you can say 'shit'."

More footsteps sounded in the hall and two paramedics came in.

"The thing is," Pete said, his voice calm and matter-of-fact, as he directed the paramedics to Williams, "we've isolated a strange drug in the blood of that poor woman whose body we found in the woods behind your house."

"One of my many houses," Williams interrupted, ignoring the man and woman examining his arm and hands. "Doesn't mean anything."

"Be that as it may, we know the woman was drugged with something the labs are busy trying to identify. And coincidentally we discovered this formula for a special drug in her files. Something new. Now, I really don't like coincidences, so I'm speculating that the formula on her computer will match up to the drug in her body. But the funny thing is, we haven't found the actual drug anywhere. Just the formula. So, say, and again I'm just speculating here, but say if that drug was to be found in that syringe, it would have been impossible for us to plant it. Interesting bit of information, isn't it?"

Williams' face turned red, but he kept quiet as the medics carefully led him to the door.

"I'll meet you at the hospital for your statement, Mr. Williams," Pete said. "I suggest you have your lawyers present." To the uniforms, he said, "Please inform Mr. Williams of his rights on the way to the hospital. We'll be charging him with breaking and entering, aggravated assault, attempted kidnapping, and intent to use a deadly weapon. For now."

Williams snorted a defiant grunt over his shoulder. "This isn't over," he said, staring directly at Sarah. "Do you hear me?"

"Threatening us in front of cops? Again?" Daniel asked, his voice even and steady. "That's on the record. Seems to me if we were to be attacked, or anything happened to us, you'd be top of the suspect list."

"That he would," Pete confirmed.

"Besides," Daniel said, "if you come after us again, broken bones will be the least of your worries."

"You heard that, too," Williams said. "He threatened *me*."

"Hmm?" Pete blinked. "Heard what?"

Williams spewed curses as the medics led him to the elevator, the two uniforms following.

"Now," Pete said, facing Daniel. "Want to explain your side of the story?"

"Not much to explain. He broke in, threatened us, tried to kidnap Sarah. We fought back."

Pete looked between her and Daniel before saying, "Broke his hands and an arm. I imagine that's some martial arts skills, huh?"

Sarah exchanged a look with Daniel and then nodded. "That's right. I've taken a few self-defense classes."

"Mm hm. And you're prepared to file a report against Mr. Williams?"

Again she looked to Daniel. The elders were going to hate this. A lot. Being questioned by the police ranked right up there on the list of things *not* to do when trying to avoid attention from the human population.

Daniel said, "Any way we can avoid filing a report, Pete?"

"Nope. Unless you want that man on the streets again by nightfall. As it is, we'll have trouble keeping him in a cell. Without a report and formal charges from you, his lawyers might be able to get that syringe tossed, despite the threats I heard." Pete looked between them again. "You all want to tell me how you know Mr. Williams?"

Sarah shook her head. She really didn't. But Williams would spin their acquaintance and "date" in his favor. If she tried to hide it, she'd look suspect. "We went on a date, about a week ago."

Pete frowned and stared at Daniel. "Your fiancée went on a date with Mr. Williams, and a week later, he's breaking into her place?"

"She was trying to make me jealous," Daniel said. "I hadn't proposed yet." He shrugged. "It worked. I proposed. Maybe Williams didn't like being dumped."

Sarah hid her smile at his story. He was very quick on his feet. Probably came with the job.

"Okay. I'll allow that for now. Anything else you want to tell me?"

"We'd like to stay as much off the radar as possible," Daniel said. "We'll press charges, but it'd be nice if the focus shifted away from us."

"That right?" Pete's gaze narrowed, suspicion clear. "What are we gonna find if we dig deeper into all this, Dan?"

"Can't say."

"Can't or won't?"

"Can't say," Daniel repeated.

Pete scowled. "All right. Come down to the station. Cooperate, file the complaint, press charges. I've got to get to the hospital. We'll talk at the station."

"We will. Thanks for everything, Pete."

"Think probably, based on what I walked in on, Mr. Williams should be thanking me. I imagine a few more things might have gotten broken otherwise."

Neither she nor Daniel commented.

Pete waved over his shoulder as he walked out the door, but before Sarah could cross to close it, he poked his head back in. "Oh, by the way, congratulations on the engagement."

"Thanks." She smiled as Pete tipped an invisible hat at her and left. She closed the door and locked it, then faced Daniel.

"Will the elders punish us for this?" she asked. "We're attracting a *lot* of attention now. And they're going to find out I was friends with a murder victim whose body went missing. I'm not sure we can avoid that."

"We won't offer it up. We shouldn't have any reason to link that death to Williams so there's no need to mention the friendship. If *they* make the link between Su-jin and Williams, well, that's another thing entirely."

"Even if they have no evidence to use?"

"It'll just add to their suspicions and encourage them to look deeper into Williams."

"Okay." She nodded. "And the elders?"

"A man attacked you while you were carrying one of our precious babies, and we defended ourselves without killing him. They don't have anything they can punish us for. We didn't break any tiger laws."

She knew that. Still…"What if Williams' lawyers dig into our lives? What if they find something?"

Daniel shrugged. "Love, we've spent centuries hiding our natures from humans while still living and working alongside them. His lawyers won't find anything we don't want them to find. Without physical proof that we're different, they have nothing to uncover. And they'd only be able to go after that physical evidence if we'd actually killed him."

"The blood…"

"Yeah, that's already disappeared."

"What?" She closed the space between them. "When?"

"Very early this morning. That's what I was talking to Alexis about earlier. She decided not to wait and risk the elders finding out about the blood. Since it's not part of the immediate investigation, though, it should take time before the police realize the samples are gone."

"Wow. She works fast."

"Yes, she does."

Sarah wrapped her arms around his neck, worry still nagging her, but being in Daniel's arms helped. "Still…This is some serious unwanted attention."

"We have a cop as witness to Williams' attack. He overheard the man threatening us. Even if you have to go to court—a little pregnant woman who looks significantly more delicate than she is?" He shook his head. "We'll be okay, Sarah. I've been upholding our laws for the last eight years. We haven't broken any of them. We haven't even broken any human laws. You're allowed to defend yourself in your own home." He hugged her tight. "I promise. We'll be fine."

Sarah nodded and tucked her head under his chin. "Okay. I trust you." And she did. With her life. With her future. With her heart. "I love you."

"I love you, too." He settled his hand over her stomach. "And if that man gets anywhere near us again, I will damage him severely."

"I'll help."

"That was a good idea, breaking bits of him without actually killing him." He kissed her temple. "Was it hard? Not killing him."

"Not as hard as I thought it would be. I was too intent on protecting our future. It wasn't about revenge in those moments, just keeping him from hurting our baby."

"Our baby. Our baby has an excellent mother."

"A very good daddy, too," she said and rose up to kiss him on the mouth.

As soon as she tasted him, their kiss turned serious. All the stress of the last few minutes, all the anxiety and anger morphed into a need to assure herself Daniel was whole and they were both okay. She wove her fingers through his hair and held him close, kissing him hard, letting her tension go.

Need rose to replace the tension she'd felt. She couldn't get him naked fast enough.

Daniel pulled her close, flattening her breasts against his chest. His heart hammered. He was alive. Safe.

Hers.

Desperate to touch him, she ripped at his t-shirt until the material hung in shredded strands across his broad shoulders.

He released his hold on her long enough for the material to drop away before pulling her close again. But her bra was still in the way. Annoyed, she jerked at the back strap, breaking the tiny hooks. A little wiggle and the material dropped to the floor between them. Once her breasts were pressed against his bare chest, all was right in Sarah's world.

She nudged him back. "Into the bedroom," she said. "I have plans for you."

"Yes," he growled, and picked her up, carrying her into her cheerful room and dropping her gently onto the large bed. "Finish stripping," he said, his gaze hot on her body.

She smiled and slowly pushed her jeans and underwear off in one swipe, then settled back on the mattress, watching him remove the rest of his clothes. She purred in the back of her throat when he stood naked before her, his beautiful cock hard and ready. But as she leaned forward to take hold of him, he shook his head.

"I need to taste you," he said and nudged her back onto the bed.

Then he leaned between her legs and licked her before she had a chance to catch her breath. The feel of his mouth on her clit, so hot and wet and perfect, sent her senses careening. Their individual scents swirled around them and joined, creating that delectable flavor that was only theirs. She moaned and fisted her hands in his hair.

"I love the sound of your pleasure," he said against her heat. "I had plans to wake you up just this way last night."

"What stopped you?" she panted. Her hips jerked when he tongued her clit before answering.

"Our unexpected visitors." His hands flexed on her thighs. "But I intend to take the very next opportunity I get."

"Oh, god, yes." She'd be more than willing to sleep a little longer if it meant waking up like this.

He licked and sucked her most sensitive flesh until she trembled. And when she couldn't hold back anymore, she let go, coming with a cry, her body beyond her control.

Before she'd fully recovered, she said, "In me. Now."

To her pleasure, he didn't hesitate. Her body still throbbed when he slid into her, his cock hard and thick. She arched to take him deeper, her every nerve alive with sensation. The friction so soon after her orgasm quickly sent her climbing to another. She let go, kissing him, her fingers digging into his back as he thrust her back over that edge.

As soon as her orgasm eased, she opened her eyes and watched him take his pleasure. His jaw tightened, his chest and shoulder muscles strained as he held himself over her. His eyes were so brilliantly blue, she practically felt a sizzle of lightning in the room.

She gripped his ass muscles and flexed her hips, the change in position breaking his control.

Sweat trickled down his temples as he pounded hard and fast into her. Then he threw his head back as he came. She held him and savored the view.

Once he gained his breath, he eased down beside her and rolled her onto her side. He set a hand low on her abdomen, frowning a little. "I don't want to risk hurting you and the baby by putting too much weight on you."

"We still have months before we need to worry about that."

"I just don't want to take any chances," he said with a stubborn jerk of his chin.

"I didn't realize how overprotective you were going to be."

"Get used to it. You think I'm protective now, just wait until you start showing."

She cupped his cheek as her heart swelled. "Daniel, your job, the future…I can handle all of it as long as I have you by my side. I love you so much. I don't really know how to express it."

He held her for a few more quiet moments, then sighed. "We'd better call the elders again and warn them what's coming with Williams and the cops." He levered up on one elbow and stared down at her. "Then we can make plans."

"For how to deal with Williams' threats?" She didn't want to think of the crazy man while she had Daniel in her bed, but they did have to be realistic about the threat he might still pose.

Daniel gave her a funny look. "Plans for our wedding."

"Oh!" She smiled. "You're not worried about his threats? What if he gets out on bail? What if he comes back?"

"We'll break him. He gets anywhere near you ever again, and he'll pray we kill him."

"Are we going to have to keep looking over our shoulders for the rest of our lives?"

"No."

"It's not going to be that simple."

"Life never is, but we'll be fine." He cupped her cheeks. "If you're worried, we'll move to India and live with my mother's family. There's a Chernikov lab there, too, so you won't have to give up your work. Besides, you're about to have a baby. The elders will bring their full power down to keep you safe."

"I'm not going to run away from that man." She pulled in a deep breath and snuggled close to Daniel, tucking her head under his chin. "It's good to know we have options, though, and that we'll have the elders' backing." She gave his ass a little squeeze. "Now about those wedding plans. I was thinking… big."

"Anything you want, love." He kissed her temple. "I'll leave the details to you."

"You sure you trust me to take care of all that?"

"I trust you period."

"You do? Even after…?"

"Yes. I won't say my trust wasn't tested. But I do trust you, Sarah. With everything I have and everything I am."

She pulled back so she could see his eyes. "With your heart?"

"Especially my heart."

She smiled and then she kissed him, her own heart full, her soul satisfied. In the back of her mind, she heard Su-jin laughing and cheering them on.

Read on for an excerpt from

HERE THERE BE TIGERS

(Tiger Shifters 3)

CHAPTER ONE

Nila DeLuca dug through her backpack in search of her cell phone as she waited by the luggage carousel for her duffle. Exhaustion weighed heavily on her limbs after the long flight from India to New York. All she could think about was dropping into the spare bed at her grandmother's house and sleeping for the next three days. She'd have to get back to work after that—there was a leopard in a Texas zoo due to give birth in a few weeks, and since big cats were her specialty, the resident vet wanted Nila on hand because of anticipated complications. Until then, she was off duty.

She yawned, still pawing through her backpack for her phone as luggage started coming through the carousel chute. She was so worn out that when she felt the hard jab of a blunt object against her ribcage, she didn't instantly react.

Then a quiet, deep voice whispered close to her ear, "Stay calm, do exactly what I say, and I won't shoot you."

Fear and confusion shot a jolt of adrenaline through her. She glanced down. Hidden from the rest of the room by her backpack was the business end of a very ugly looking gun. She swallowed hard and tried not to panic, but her heartbeat tripled and her breathing sped.

"What do you want?" she murmured, carefully lowering her bag. She didn't want to make any abrupt moves, but someone else in the crowded JFK luggage area *had* to notice a friggin' gun.

To her dismay, the barrel shifted to her lower back and she felt the man move closer behind her, no doubt covering his weapon.

"If you cooperate," he said against her ear, "you might survive this. If you resist, I'll kill you first, then hunt down Leo and Rossa and kill them. And I'll make sure their deaths are slow and painful."

"Why?" she hissed as another spike of panic shot through her. Her father and grandmother were her only close family. Why would anyone want to hurt them?

She tried getting a look at her the man from the corner of her eye, but he wasn't leaning far enough forward for her to even glimpse a hair color.

"Someone would like to talk to you," he said, putting his free arm around her waist. To strangers, it probably looked like a hug from a boyfriend.

"Listen, buddy," she said, "I think you've got the wrong person. I'm just a vet. Unless you've got a big cat in need of medical help, I'm of no use to you. And if you do have a big cat that needs a vet, you just have to ask."

His chuckle sent a shiver across her shoulders. The fine hairs on her arms rose.

"We'll have to see what he says, won't we?" the man said. "But he might let you live if you prove useful."

This made no sense. She hated when things didn't make sense. It drove her crazy. The pet peeve sparked irritation that quickly turned to anger. "If you think you're gonna sell me into some form of white slavery, don't bother. I'm a ball buster."

"Oh, I have no doubt you are. Let's go." He nudged her hard with the gun.

She sucked in a breath. "What about my luggage?" She spotted her duffle dropping down the ramp.

"Won't need it."

He butted her again with the gun, and she either had to move or risk being shot. To buy herself some thinking time, she walked slowly with a limp.

"What are you doing? Move it."

"I can't, damn it. I hurt my ankle a few days ago. It's still killing me."

"Your ankle will be the least of your worries if you don't move faster."

His response told her two things: he hadn't seen her walk into the luggage area, because she was lying through her teeth about the injury, and he was afraid of getting caught. That last part was good for her. She just had to find a way to attract the attention of someone who could help without getting anyone in the area killed.

Even as that thought crossed her mind, she passed a small family, the youngest child pulling at his mother's skirt from his stroller.

Fuck. There were *too* many people in here. That should have worked in her favor. Someone should see the gun. But no one seemed to notice anything beyond their own baggage hunt. If she called attention to her abduction, the man might start shooting innocent people.

"Where are we going?" she asked, still limping to stall their progress.

"Parking lot. Then a short drive."

She was very certain she wouldn't survive getting into a car with this man. Who the hell was he? Why on earth would he kidnap her? He had to know who she was because he knew her father and grandmother's names. Yet she wasn't rich, she didn't have the kind of job that inspired kidnappings, and she was pretty sure she wasn't actually attractive enough for the sex slave market. So, what the hell was going on?

When they stepped through the sliding doors into a muggy New York August night, she caught a brief glimpse of the gunman in the glass door—dark hair and eyes, pale skin, a dark, short sleeved shirt, taller than her 5'3" height by almost a foot. The doors had opened too fast for her to see more than that.

She chanced a downward glance. The arm still around her waist was covered in dark hair and well-muscled. Those muscles were relaxed but felt coiled and ready to react if she so much as breathed the wrong way.

He nudged her in one direction just as another man hurried up to them.

"Taxi? Taxi, sir? Going into the city?"

She tried catching the man's gaze to let him see her distress, but his full focus was on the man behind her.

"Get out of my face," the kidnapper spat.

"Hey, no need to be rude." The driver raised his hands in surrender. "Just offering."

The cab driver glanced down at her. And winked. She had just enough time to frown. In the next instant, the driver pushed her to one side, the surprise move freeing her from the gunman's hold. She stumbled away as a low growl from behind her raised the hairs on her arms. Before she caught her balance, she heard a painful sounding crunch, then the driver had her elbow, maneuvering her away from the kidnapper. She glanced back long enough to see the other man holding his wrist. He looked up, glaring after her with eyes that seemed to glow yellow.

She sucked in a sharp breath and turned away when he started toward them.

"He's coming," she said.

"Let's move."

The driver tugged her into a trot, then into a full run.

She threw her backpack over her free shoulder and did her best to keep up as they wove through the throngs of people on the sidewalk. He rushed her toward the parking lot, ducking around the long line waiting for a taxi.

"Whoa, wait." She tried nudging his big body back toward the luggage area. "We have to go to airport security." Panic continued to shoot adrenaline through her blood stream, mixing badly with her confusion.

"Security can't help with that guy," the driver said without altering his direction.

"And you can? Who are you?" She wanted to slow down so they could talk, though she didn't dare stop moving.

A quick glance confirmed the gunman was still behind them. Fortunately, he was caught up in a tangled mass of people and luggage but that wouldn't delay him for long. Her rescuer urged her to a quicker trot, pulling her attention back to where she was going. She looked longingly at the nearest entrance into the airport, wondering where to find a security person.

"I'm a friend of your grandmother's," the man said. "Rossa sent me."

Startled, she tripped on an uneven section of concrete. He caught her before she fell, helping her regain her footing with surprising strength and ease.

"You can trust me." He held her gaze for a heartbeat.

The brief look stunned her to silence. His expression was hard and serious, his eyes intent. He was also probably the most handsome man she'd ever seen, now that she stopped to actually look. Short, shaggy brown hair, light eyes, classically handsome features.

But it was the hum of her instincts giving her pause. Those same instincts had served her well her entire life, keeping her safe in her travels around the world and helping her work with injured, angry cats that could outweighed her by two hundred pounds or more. Now, her instincts were whispering that the man before her was saving her life.

Trust him.

Her quick, certain insight got brushed to the back of her mind as he pulled her into a run toward the parking lot.

"You know my grandmother?" she said as she tried to breathe and run at the same time.

"I'll tell you everything when we're safe. This way." He led her between the rows of cars, down a ramp to a lower level, then up another row of cars.

"That man was trying to get me to the parking lot."

"Probably because he has a car here, too."

"Are you working with him?"

"No."

She tried getting a look at his face, but he was a step ahead of her so she couldn't see his expression. Her instincts continued urging her to trust him.

The skin between her shoulder blades crawled with the knowledge that the gunman was still somewhere behind them. The man beside her didn't give her the willies like the other man did. Hell, this guy had stopped her kidnapping, and he claimed to know her grandmother. He knew her grandmother's name. Though, so had the kidnapper.

But since she didn't feel the need to get away from this man, and he was making sure she did get away from the man with the gun, she decided to listen to her instincts. "You're not a taxi driver are you?"

"No."

This time, she heard a hint of humor in his voice. "That man's still following us."

"I know. We're almost safe."

"Right." Unintended sarcasm slipped into her tone.

He flashed her a half-smile that nearly made her stumble again. Holy hell. When he smiled, he was stunning, even in the awful, overly bright parking lot lighting. How was that even possible?

She decided adrenaline was warping her sense of reality and shook off the strange effect the man's smile had on her. She had more important things to do just then. Like survive.

"You know what that other guy wants from me?" She panted, stretching to keep up with his longer strides.

"Yes. We'll discuss it later."

"We need to go to the police."

"He has people inside the NYPD."

"My kidnapper?" That seemed…extreme.

"His boss."

She wanted to ask more but he shoved her in front of him and she heard a beep beep as car door locks opened. He led her to the passenger side of a large, black SUV.

"Get in."

She didn't bother arguing. She could do that later when she no longer felt the other man hunting them. That was the only way to describe it. She couldn't hear him or see him anymore, but she knew her kidnapper was still back there...somewhere. Fear tingled along the back of her neck.

She held her breath while her rescuer hurried to the driver's side, climbed in and locked the doors. She started breathing again when he backed out of the parking spot and pulled away. She still couldn't see the other man.

"Did you break his wrist?" she asked as she scoured the area for any sign of the kidnapper.

"Yes."

"Where's his gun?"

He handed her the weapon, grip first. "Now, duck down. Just in case."

After one last glance around the parking lot, she did as he suggested. She hated guns, so she checked the safety, then set the weapon on the floor, stepping on it to keep it from sliding under the seat. She couldn't stand having a gun in her hands. The feel of them disgusted her.

The fact that he'd handed her the gun had gone a long way toward confirming her instinctive reaction to trust him. But now she wanted answers. Who was he? How did he know her grandmother? What the hell was going on?

"You're going to answer my questions when we're safe, right?" she said from her undignified crouch. She had to concentrate on not throwing up as the adrenaline took its toll.

"Probably." He glanced down and smiled again, the look quick and lethally sexy. Then he returned to focusing on his driving. "My name is Mikhail Chernikov, by the way. Call me

Mitch or Michael. I hate Mikhail. Only my grandmother calls me that. And it's a pleasure to meet you, Nila."

His last name sounded vaguely familiar. Where had she heard it before? When her memory failed her, she gave up and asked, "Where are we going?"

"Somewhere safe."

"Is there a reason I'm trusting you?"

"I just saved your life?"

Nila let out a long, slow sigh. "That's what I thought."

*** Here There Be Tigers (Tiger Shifters 3) ***
*** AVAILABLE NOW! ***

About the Author

Kat Simons earned her Ph.D in animal behavior, working with animals as diverse as dolphins and deer. She brought her experience and knowledge of biology to her paranormal romance fiction, where she delights in taking nature and turning it on its ear. After traveling the world, she now lives in New York City with her family. Kat is a stay-at-home mom and a full time writer.

For more on Kat and her future books:

Website: http://www.katsimons.com
Newsletter: http://eepurl.com/OxQQL

TITLES BY KAT SIMONS

Tiger Shifters Series

ONCE UPON A TIGER
ALONG CAME A TIGER
HERE THERE BE TIGERS
HER TIGER TO TAKE
TO TEMPT A TIGER
DOWN WILL COME TIGER